D0456222

People or Monsters?

CHINESE LITERATURE IN TRANSLATION

Editors
Irving Yucheng Lo
Joseph S. M. Lau
Leo Ou-fan Lee
Eugene Chen Eoyang

PEOPLE *OR* MONSTERS?

And Other Stories and Reportage from China after Mao

LIU BINYAN

Edited by

Perry Link

INDIANA UNIVERSITY PRESS
Bloomington

First Midland Book Edition 1983

Copyright © 1983 by Indiana University Press

Manufactured in the United States of America

Library of Congress Cataloging in Publication Data

Liu, Pin-yen, 1925–
  People or monsters?

  (Chinese literature in translation)
  Contents: Introduction / by Leo Ou-fan Lee—Listen
carefully to the voice of the people / translated by
Kyna Rubin and Perry Link—People or monsters? / trans-
lated by James V. Feinerman, with Perry Link—[etc.]
  I. Link, E. Perry (Eugene Perry), 1944–
II. Title. III. Series.
PL2879.P5A26   1984   895.1'35   82-48594
ISBN 0-253-34329-1
ISBN 0-253-20313-9 (pbk.)
2 3 4 5 6 92 91 90 89 88

Contents

SOUND IS BETTER THAN SILENCE
Translated by Michael S. Duke

CONTRIBUTORS

Editor's Note

This book was conceived during the editing of *Stubborn Weeds: Chinese Literature after the Cultural Revolution* (Indiana University Press, 1983), where "People or Monsters?" "Warning," and "The Fifth Man in the Overcoat" were originally set to appear. In discussions with the Press it emerged that a writer as incisive as Liu Binyan, and as widely respected both inside and outside China, deserves a separate volume. I am grateful to the Press for supporting this idea, as well as to the Committee on Scholarly Communication with the People's Republic of China, who sponsored the research stay in China during which I began the project. I am indebted to my colleagues who helped flesh out the volume on very short notice: to Leo Ou-fan Lee for his introduction, to Michael S. Duke for translating "Sound is Better than Silence" with astounding dispatch, and to Kyna Rubin for locating an authentic text of "Listen Carefully to the Voice of the People." I also offer my sincere thanks to James V. Feinerman, Madelyn Ross, and John S. Rohsenow for tolerating my extensive, not to say picayune, tamperings with their draft translations.

Liu Binyan was not consulted about this book and bears no responsibility for its conception or the selection of pieces.

Introduction

LEO OU-FAN LEE

Among the Chinese writers who have emerged or reemerged since the downfall of the Gang of Four in 1976, Liu Binyan occupies a unique position. By profession a practicing journalist, Liu is a writer of major stature who was recently elected to the board of directors and the secretariat of the Chinese Writers Associaton. He was a "star" participant at the Fourth Congress of Writers and Artists (October 30–November 16, 1979) and gave one of the best-received speeches at the Third Congress of the Chinese Writers Association. A rehabilitated Party member, he is also the most outspoken critic of Party bureaucracy. His Chinese readers throughout China and abroad, communists and noncommunists alike, know him as a man of great integrity and one of the leading voices of social conscience on the post-Mao literary scene.

Liu's own biographical background shows a typical "personal history" of a "true believer" victimized by the vicissitudes of political movements. Born in 1925 in Jilin Province in the Northeastern region, he received poor schooling because of the Japanese invasion following the Mukden Incident on September 8, 1931. But he later managed to teach himself Russian, Japanese, and a bit of English. He joined the underground activities of the Chinese Communist Party in 1943 and soon became a Party member. In 1951, he was transferred to Beijing and worked as a reporter and editor at the Party newspaper, *Zhongguo qingnian bao* (The Chinese youth). In 1956, responding to Mao Zedong's call for free criticism in the "Hundred Flowers" movement, he published three works in which he attacked the bureaucratic style of Party cadres. As a result, in the subsequent "Anti-Rightist" campaign, he was branded a "rightist" and a representative of "anti-Party adverse current," his works, "poisonous weeds," and he was "sent down" to various localities in the Chinese countryside for labor reform from 1958 to 1961. In 1961, he went back to work at his old newspaper as a researcher-translator for eight years. Following the outbreak of the Cultural Revolution, he was again sent down to attend the so-called May Seventh cadre schools from 1969 to 1977. Finally, after twenty-one years of enforced silence, he was rehabilitated in 1979. His current position is with the official newspaper, *The People's Daily.*

The formidable reputation that Liu now enjoys has been earned chiefly by a single work, a lengthy piece of reportage titled "People or Monsters?" (Renyao zhi jian), which upon its publication in September 1979 created an immediate sensation in China. Some of the high-ranking cadres felt scandalized by his unstinting exposé. On the other hand, enthusiastic letters poured in from every province except Tibet. This *vox populi* has given vivid testimony not only to the profound impact Liu's reportage has exerted but also to its broad, representative significance. The corruption depicted therein of a middle-aged female cadre by the name of Wang Shouxin in a small county in the remote Heilongjiang Province of northeastern China is certainly not an isolated case, but a nationwide phenomenon. The following letter from a worker is quoted by Liu in his article "The Call of the Times":

> When I read your "People or Monsters?" an indescribable force caused me to crush the glass in my hand to pieces. Glass splinters lacerated my palm, but I felt no pain. In fact, it brought a sensation of euphoria.
>
> Your pen wove a net over Binxian, but why stop there? The characters you wrote of are not peculiar to Binxian, are they? To put it bluntly, it is a microcosm of the whole country and describes a force that is obstructing the Four Modernizations, a force whose defeat is urgent.
>
> In study time after work, I read your "People or Monsters?" to the fourteen workers in my section in a mood of great excitement. The listeners included women with their children, busy young people, and tired old workers who had thoughts of nothing but rest. But for more than three hours of reading, not a single one left; in fact, they called more and more people over. That is how much they wanted to listen. I am not just saying this to flatter you, for that would be a waste of time. I was asked by these workers to write and congratulate you. They

wanted to express their hope that our comrade Liu Binyan will continue to tell us the truth in the future, for we no longer want to hear
any more lies or deceptions.[1]

For Western readers who do not necessarily share this "sensation
of euphoria," the piece may pose more difficulties: it is not strictly
speaking a literary work; its welter of unfamiliar names and its depic-
tions of the bureaucratic maze are not easy to digest. But as I have
argued elsewhere,[2] this is precisely the initial effect intended by the
author. As a reporter who is drawn into this case, Liu Binyan's own
reactions may have been quite similar. Like a detective, Liu finds
himself uncovering layer upon layer of bribery, corruption, backdoor-
ism, and abuse of power, with seemingly no end in sight. And he has
presented himself as an over-zealous raconteur telling his readers
what he has discovered with impetuous tempo and seeming disre-
gard for the narrative art. Once we are drawn into this "story," the
experience becomes increasingly exhilarating and, at the same time,
profoundly disturbing. For the accumulated impact of the piece is
directed ultimately at the socialist system itself. Amidst the national
celebrations that greeted the downfall of the Gang of Four, Liu Binyan alone adopted a Cassandra-like warning voice, as he intoned at
the end of "People or Monsters?":

> The case of Wang Shouxin's corruption has been cracked. But how
> many of the social conditions that gave rise to this case have really
> changed? Isn't it true that Wang Shouxins of all shapes and sizes, in all
> corners of the land, are still in place, continuing to gnaw away at
> socialism, continuing to tear at the fabric of the Party, and continuing
> to evade punishment by the dictatorship of the proletariat?
> People, be on guard! It is still too early to be celebrating victories . . .

Such a somber tone and devastating exposure of the "dark" side of
contemporary Chinese society is unprecedented in the entire corpus
of post-Liberation Chinese literature (not to mention official reportage). In the volatile atmosphere of Chinese politics, it takes not only
personal courage but selfless dedication to tell the gruesome and
unappetizing truth about contemporary Chinese society.

To speak the truth is, in fact, the reigning theme that informs Liu's
three early works published in 1956: "On the Bridge Construction
Site" (Zai qiaoliang gongdi shang), "The Inside Story of This Newspaper" (Benbao neibu xiaoxi), and its sequel.[3] While criticizing the

bureaucrats, Liu affirms the role of the reporter to speak the truth as he or she sees it. The protagonist of "The Inside Story" is, like Liu, a young reporter, Huang Jiaying, who finds her impulses to describe the reality of the situation in a coal mine contradicted by the pressures from her superiors to conform to Party directives. Huang's application to join the Communist Party is judged, ironically, according to whether or not she is willing to conform. The story ends with the Party members still deliberating over Huang's case, but the reader is left with no doubt as to the author's position: for the good of the Party and the future of the country a reporter and Party member cannot afford not to think independently and to speak the truth.

It is, from an outsider's perspective, a matter of supreme irony that such an idealistic conception born of Liu's political faith has been ill matched by the reality of the Party bureaucracy, which in fact has deteriorated since he voiced such sentiments. When he registered some soul-searching thoughts in his diary in the late 1950s, that diary was secretly copied by another Party member and later used as evidence against him. Thus in 1966, merely two months after his "rightist" cap had been lifted, a big-character poster from this comrade recharged him as an "anti-Party rightist."

Liu's speech "Listen Carefully to the Voice of the People" is poignant testimony to his personal experience and his mental struggle to reform according to the injunctions from the Party. Yet the result of his prolonged soul-searching is that if he must choose between two versions of truth—the consistently rosy "official" version and the painful version related to him by local peasants—he would rather side with that of the people. Consequently, Liu's sense of realism is itself a defiant stance; it is burdened with an ethical weight accumulated from twenty-one years of experience and reflection. As practiced in his own writing, this ethical sense of realism is translated into his famous motto to have literature "delve into life" (*ganyu shenghuo*)—that is, the writer must *actively* render a truthful reflection of the reality of life so that it, in turn, exerts a powerful impact on the actual life of the readers.[4] In adopting this stance of committed writing, Liu has made himself vulnerable to criticism from two different camps: he has been accused by the more ideological "Left" of being too excessively concerned with the darker aspects of Chinese society, which of course is contrary to Mao's injunction to "extol" revolutionary reality. On the other hand, from the more artistically oriented

writers comes the critique that Liu is too didactic, that he still wishes
to use literature as a tool for political persuasion and not as art. In a
sense they are both correct. However, they have failed to grasp the
unique significance of Liu's work and the real objectives of his "meth-
odology."

As Liu himself states, his motto "delve into life" is "aimed at the
tendency in literature and art to evade the contradictions and conflicts
in reality and to cosmetize life" *(fenshi shenghuo).*[5] Such a tendency
has, of course, characterized Chinese writing ever since Chairman
Mao gave his famous Talks at the Yan'an Forum on Literature and Art
in 1942. This Maoist canon of literature in the service of revolutionary
politics has shaped and dominated the consciousness of Chinese
writers for the past three decades. After Mao's death in 1976, a
nationwide reaction against his Cultural Revolution policies triggered
a reaction against his literary doctrine as well. As the tremendous
volume of works published since 1977 has shown, the basic tenor of
this new writing is dark exposure, focusing not only on the wrongdoing of the Gang of Four (as in the so-called scar literature around
1977–78) but also on the variegated ills of a problem-ridden society.
Liu's "People or Monsters?", published when the literary thaw was at
its most advanced, thus exemplifies and sets a new standard of this
exposure ethos, for it towers above all previous works in its devastating probing of a deep-seated evil nurtured in the very "body politic"
of the socialist system.

In the post-thaw context of the early 1980s, however, Liu's daring
stance hangs in the balance between moderation and a new radical
reaction against moderation. The official position of the Party, as
reflected by Hu Yaobang's recent speeches, is intriguing. Hu has
warned against excessive exposure of social ills and the tendency of
"bourgeois liberalization"; at the same time, the Party seems to give
tacit consent to the new strain of artistic experimentation (represented by the works of Wang Meng and others) that deemphasizes
the sociopolitical functions of literature. The unfolding of the new
official policy seems to favor writings of the more artistic variety that
are politically innocuous and ideologically safe, whereas artistically
inferior but politically sensitive or sensational works—such as Bai
Hua's screenplay "Unrequited Love" (Kulian)[6] and the works by
younger writers of the "unofficial journals"—have been either se-
verely criticized or banned. Liu Binyan's reportage belongs ultimately

in the "political" variety, and we have reason to believe that, without behind-the-scenes protection from Hu Yaobang himself, Liu would have been the easy target of another pseudo-campaign (since the leadership has formally declared an end to all political campaigns) comparable to the Bai Hua case.

Liu Binyan has acknowledged that he is hopelessly lacking in the power of imagination because as a reporter he must deal with "real people and real events." He does not like "fabrication" and would rather seek out truth from the material of genuine life so as to achieve the result of fact speaking more eloquently than fiction.[7] Thus in describing the case of Wang Shouxin, he does not wish to write a literary work but an "investigative report." Because of his declared intentions, two Chinese terms have been applied to his writing: *"texie"* and *"baogao wenxue."* The former term, which may be translated as "special feature," or "sketch," may have been derived from the Russian term "ocherk," which in turn was originally taken from the French term *"esquisse physiologique."*[8] Used first in the eighteenth century, it was a kind of report on the "physiological" environment of the "masses" by an intellectual writer and commentator. When Liu talks about the need for "sociology," he has in mind not necessarily the current American definitions of the discipline but rather a kind of *"esquisse,"* statistically detailed, on a segment of society—be it a factory, commune, or county. For him, the lack of such a "sociology" explains the regime's inability to solve problems that in a big country like China have become increasingly complex. Liu once told me that his ambition was to do a series of such "sociological sketches." But as a Chinese critic has pointed out, there may be two subcategories of *texie*, and Liu has clearly adopted in his "People or Monsters?" the type of "literary sketch" *(wenxue texie)* that gives the writer more flexibility to reorganize his material without the restrictions of "journalistic sketch" *(xinwen texie)*, which is more objective but also more passive.[9] Thus, Liu's reportage can also be taken as a special kind of proto-literary writing; hence the term "reportage literature" *(baogao wenxue)*. But the phrase likewise places more emphasis on "reportage," which is closely linked with sociological investigation *(diaocha)*, than on "literature" per se. Since Communist China has had until recently no proper sociology to speak of, the responsibility seems to fall on the shoulders of Liu's ideal reporter, who investigates and reports truthfully a social situation. In other words, the role of the journalist in Liu's conception certainly goes beyond that of a passive "newspaperman," someone who works for a newspaper (which in the People's Republic is invariably an official organ). Liu's model journalist is by definition actively and ethically involved in sociological investigation. In both *texie* and *baogao wenxue*, the intrusive presence of the reporter/writer is assumed, although it is in the service of a larger purpose and not merely to embellish his own ego (as found in some of the eminent practitioners of American New Journalism). Moreover, the investigation is avowedly focused on problems and problem solving; hence the necessary connection with exposure. It is also by necessity "realistic" literature.

But as specimens of literature Liu's reportage pieces are faulty because his reorganizations and stylistic inventions are not generated by artistic concerns intrinsic to the text itself; they are, on the other hand, aimed at generating maximum audience response. The ultimate goal of Liu's "delving into life" is to invite his audience to "delve" into their own lives as well; otherwise, no problem uncovered can be resolved. Therefore, by the conventional standards of literary criticism, "People or Monsters?" is by no means a masterpiece.[10] The proper gauge of its value lies not only in the truthfulness of its content but also in audience impact. In this regard it is an unqualified, and as yet unrivaled, success. Since "People or Monsters?", Liu has written several similar pieces of reportage, but for some reason they are not as overpowering. The other piece included in this volume, "Sound Is Better than Silence," is carefully crafted and no doubt based on a real figure who played "dumb" for twelve years. If it were fiction, a novelist of Wang Meng's caliber could surely turn the middle part of the story into some "stream-of-consciousness" revelation of the protagonist's inner turmoil during the Cultural Revolution. The motif of the feigned physical defect also offers rich possibilities for psychological and allegorical treatments, examples of which abound in modern Western literature. (For instance, Günter Grass might in fact find Liu's sketch very appealing when compared with *The Tin Drum*, in which the protagonist, instead of playing dumb, refuses to grow up.) But because of his commitments to this special genre, Liu has willingly forsaken art in favor of truth and reality.

It is only when Liu is confronted with material that obviously falls outside the realm of reality that he resorts, rather crudely, to "fiction." The story "Warning" deals with ghosts, which certainly cannot be dealt with through reportage. It is also likely that the last unnamed "ghost" in the story refers to a real political figure—in my conjecture Kang Sheng, a leader of the Cultural Revolution group and widely rumored to be a cruel "executioner." A "fictional" format is needed for purposes of safety. (Some of the names in "People or Monsters?" are also altered for the same reason.) But fiction is clearly subsidiary to reportage in Liu's scale. "The Fifth Man in the Overcoat," billed as a short story, betrays strong traces of reportage. As in "The Inside Story of This Newspaper," the protagonist is a reporter who is intent on finding out the facts behind a case of wrongdoing. Interestingly, both stories are "fiction" about truth. The only difference between the earlier and later stories seems to be that the author is now less idealistic and more sullen than before. Behind the obvious themes of truth and justice in "The Fifth Man" lurks the disquieting motif of evil and its invincibility. Although the case of Wang Shouxin has been solved in real life, the fictional figure of He Qixiong in "The Fifth Man," who has masterminded several plots to implicate innocent people, causing divorce, insanity, and death, continues to rise in his political fortune. It is perhaps this final "realism," the reluctant realization that the forces of evil and injustice may not ultimately be defeated because of the omnipresence of people—or monsters—like Wang Shouxin and He Qixiong, which imparts a degree of tragic irony to Liu Binyan's warning: "People, be on guard! It is still too early to celebrate victories." In a country and a literature that for thirty years have shown little tragic sense of life, Liu Binyan's voice is all the more precious and deserves to be heard.

That Liu is allowed to continue with his writing may be an indication of the Party's more relaxed policy. It also reflects, more importantly, Liu's own commitment to the act of writing itself. After two decades of silence, there is an almost existential ring to his remark that, having gone this far, "there is no way back": "I thought it over and decided that I had to speak out. If I didn't, then what was I doing back in the Party? What would it mean then to be a communist? What would my life mean?"[11] It is statements like these, which signify a rare combination of pessimism and affirmation, of despair and commitment, that invest Liu Binyan's spirit of integrity with a depth of humanity reminiscent of Lu Xun, modern China's foremost writer and intellectual. Even if Liu were never to produce another work comparable to "People or Monsters?", his preeminence as a defiant figure in the Chinese Communist Party and as a writer of conscience is assured. We can only hope that Liu Binyan will continue to speak out, unhampered, through his writing.

NOTES

1. Liu Binyan, "Shidai de zhaohuan" (The call of the times), English translation by John Beyer in Howard Goldblatt ed., *Chinese Literature for the 1980s: The Fourth Congress of Writers and Artists* (Armonk, N.Y.: M. E. Sharpe, 1982), p. 118.
2. See my article in Chinese, "Liu Binyan he 'Renyao zhijian'" (Liu Binyan and "People or Monsters?"), *Qishi niandai* (The seventies, Hong Kong), no. 129 (Oct. 1980), pp. 79–82.
3. These three pieces are included in *Liu Binyan baogao wenxue xuan* (Selections from Liu Binyan's reportage literature) (Beijing: Beijing chuban she, 1981), pp. 25–146.
4. For Liu's views on this subject, see his "Guanyu 'xie yin'an mian' he 'ganyu shenghuo'" (Concerning "exposing the dark side" and "delving into life"), in Huang Dazhi, ed., *Zhongguo xin xieshi zhuyi wenyi pinglun xuan—Liu Binyan ji qi zuopin* (Selected literary criticism from Chinese neo-realism—Liu Binyan and his works) (Hong Kong: Bowen shuju, 1980), pp. 142–49.
5. Ibid., p. 143.
6. For an analysis of Bai Hua's controversial screenplay, see Michael S. Duke, "A Drop of Spring Rain: The Sense of Humanity in Bai Hua's *Unrequited Love*," in *Chinese Literature: Essays, Articles, Reviews* (forthcoming).
7. See Liu Shaotang's comments in his open letter to Liu Binyan, in *Zhongguo xin xieshi zhuyi wenyi pinglun xuan*, pp. 200–202.
8. I am indebted to Professor Rudolph Wagner of the Free University of Berlin for bringing this to my attention. Since Liu himself reads Russian, the Russian origin of his *texie* can be ascertained.
9. Wu Wenxu, "Cong 'Zai qiaoliang gongdi shang' dao 'Renyao zhijian'" (From "On the Bridge Construction Site" to "People or Monsters?"), *Wenhui bao* (Oct. 23, 1979), p. 3.
10. For an analysis from a literary and historical angle, see Michael Duke, "Ironies of History in the Reportage Fiction of Liu Binyan," paper presented at the Conference on "Contemporary Chinese Literature: Forms of Realism?" St. John's University, New York (May 28–31, 1982).
11. Liu Binyan, "The Call of the Times," in Goldblatt, *Chinese Literature for the 1980s*, p. 119.

People or Monsters?

LISTEN CAREFULLY TO THE VOICE OF THE PEOPLE

TRANSLATED BY KYNA RUBIN AND PERRY LINK

On November 9, 1979, Liu Binyan gave a startling speech at the Fourth Congress of Chinese Literature and Art Workers in Beijing. Repeatedly interrupted by spontaneous applause, the speech eventually became famous not only as a clear exposition of key problems that had been facing Chinese writers in recent times, but also as a courageous statement of thoughts that had occurred to many intellectuals but that few had dared to mention in public.

The speech has never been published as originally spoken. Excerpts were published in People's Daily *on November 26, 1979, under the title "Listen Carefully to the Voice of the People" (Qingting renmin de shengyin). The present translation is based on this version, although we have restored some deleted lines. The* Literary Gazette *(Wenyibao), in its November–December issue of 1979 (nos. 11 and 12), published a fuller and more extensively edited version of the speech under the title "The Call of the Times" (Shidai de zhaohuan).[1]—*ED.

1. Face Life Squarely, and Listen Carefully to the Voice of the People

Of the middle-aged writers present at our Fourth Congress on Literature and Art, the most active and prolific in the past two years have been comrades such as Bai Hua, Wang Meng, Deng Youmei, Gong Liu, Shao Yanxiang, Cong Weixi, and Liu Shaotang. Considering their actual age, they should not look as old as they do.

---

1. An earlier version of the present translation will appear in a collection of translations of Chinese literature from 1979 to 1980, edited by Mason Wang (University Center, Mich.: Green River Press, 1983). The version of the speech that appears in *Literary Gazette* is translated by John Beyer in Howard Goldblatt, ed., *Chinese Literature for the 1980s* (Armonk, N.Y.: M. E. Sharpe, 1982), pp. 103–20.

Just look at Bai Hua, with his head of white hair, and Gong Liu—who has entirely lost his hair. Whose fault is this?

If mistakes have been made, I must ask why it is that scientists are permitted their mistakes, and so are politicians, while writers alone are forbidden to make mistakes. It is said that the mistakes of scientists are forgivable because they produce no "social effects";[2] but then what about the mistakes of politicians? Which is larger—the consequences of a politician's mistake or the consequences of a writer's? How many times larger?

Those of us here today are fortunate to be alive and well, to have had our "rightist" labels removed,[3] and to be able once again to serve the people with our pens. But we mustn't forget all the young people who were implicated with us twenty-two years ago. They were also labeled "rightists." Some of the verdicts on them have not been reversed even today. I am thinking of our comrade Lin Xiling, whose fate has been even worse than ours.[4] I hereby appeal to all those in authority, including the leadership of People's University, to expedite the rectification of these cases. These "rightists" have lost more than twenty of the most precious years of their lives, and don't have very many more to go. The question of their exoneration simply must not be allowed to drag on any longer.

But looking back over the last twenty or more years, I feel we have gained certain things in spite of our losses. Fate brought us into intimate contact with the lowest levels of the laboring masses; our joys and worries became for a time the same as their own. Our hopes were no different from theirs. This experience allowed us to see, to hear, and to feel for ourselves things that others have been unable to see, hear, or feel.

---

2. "Social effects" here means undesirable social consequences. The phrase has been widely used in post-Mao China to maintain a subtle yet sometimes strong pressure on writers to conform with official policy.

3. Liu refers to labels applied during the Anti-Rightest campaign of 1957, when hundreds of thousands of intellectuals who had criticized Party policies were punished for anti-Party or anti-socialist thought.

4. Lin Xiling was a young lecturer at People's University in Beijing when she was arrested in 1957 and charged with being part of the "Zhang (Bojun)–Luo (Longji) Alliance," a group who objected to the one-party system, to ignorant Party officials "leading" non-Party specialists, and to the political campaigns forced upon the nation after 1949.

In my own personal experience, the most unforgettable years were 1958–60, when I shared a bed and even sometimes a quilt with poor peasants. The things I saw in the villages, and the plaints I heard from the peasants, were all vastly different from what was being spread by the authorities and the press. Whom was I to believe? I had resolved at the time to obey the Party and to remold myself from the bone marrow outward. But there is no avoiding the fact that objective, material things are more powerful than subjective, spiritual ones. However great my will to reform, it was no match for the continual onslaught of certain plain incongruities. For example, the higher authorities told us that our impoverished gully of a village ought to build a zoo and a fountain. Now, what were peasants who hardly ate meat all year supposed to feed to lions and tigers in a zoo? With no water source—with man and beast still drinking rainwater—how were they to build a fountain? A struggle began to rage deep inside me: how could two diametrically opposed "truths" coexist in the world? The longings of the peasants were one truth, and the policies of the higher-ups and the propaganda in the newspapers were quite another. Which should I follow? Not until 1960, when Party Central issued its "Twelve Points on Rural Policy,"[5] did I finally get my answer. It was right to uphold the interests and demands of the people. Anything that ran counter to their wishes was ultimately untenable.

This year we have seen the appearance of Ru Zhijuan's "The Misedited Story" and Liu Zhen's "Black Flag," both of which are stories about these same years I have just been speaking of.[6] We should ask ourselves what the "social effects" would have been if stories like these had been permitted publication twenty-one years ago. Would the masses have risen in opposition to the Communist Party? Would the peasants have rebelled? History tells us they would not have. The effect of these short stories would have been

---

5. The "Twelve Points on Rural Policy" was an emergency classified document aimed at rectifying serious economic dislocations that had resulted from the overly idealistic policies of the Great Leap Forward in 1958–59.

6. "The Misedited Story" (Jianji cuole de gushi) was published in *People's Literature* (*Renmin wenxue*) no. 2, 1979. "Black Flag" (Heiqi) was published in *Shanghai Literature* (*Shanghai wenxue*) no. 3, 1979; an English translation appears in *Chinese Literature* (Beijing), May 1980. Both stories attack the excesses of the Great Leap Forward and the decline from previous years in the Communist Party's concern for the peasantry.

quite the opposite: they would have helped the Party to see its mistakes while there was still time to make changes. Such changes would have heightened the Party's prestige, strengthened the collective socialist economy, and stimulated the peasants both economically and politically. Recent experience has taught us time and again that true harm to the prestige of the Party and socialism is done not by literary works that describe problems, but by the problems themselves, problems that have been caused by our own mistakes and by the destructiveness of our enemies.[7] Had writers during 1958–60 been able to hold their heads high, to speak out in behalf of the people, to uncover mistakes, and to expose the destructiveness of our enemies, this would, in fact, have been the best way they could have upheld the Party and socialism. Yet in 1958 no one was writing works such as those by Liu Zhen and Ru Zhijuan, and even in 1962, when Party Central summed up the lessons of the 1958–60 period, no one could write stories that told the truth about peasant life. Not for twenty years—not until the third year after the "smashing of the Gang of Four"—did *People's Literature* and *Shanghai Literature* publish these two stories, thereby reclaiming for literature some of its rights to tell the truth about life. Even today we have to admire the political courage of these two editorial boards.

We should try to learn from our experience, and I have three points to offer in this regard.

First, writers should face life squarely and listen carefully to the voice of the people. The policies of the Party must pass the test of practice and be corrected when they are wrong. When faced with the "two kinds of truth" that I referred to a moment ago, we writers must maintain a strong sense of responsibility to the people in reaching our conclusions. Our thinking must be dead serious, never rash, and always independent. We must never simply follow the crowd. The test of time has shown that all those literary works about peasant life in the late 1950s are dead today, whereas stories like those by Liu Zhen and Ru Zhijuan live on.

Second, some comrades apparently feel that literature's "delving

---

7. "Enemies" here refers to the domestic enemies who conceived and directed the Great Leap Forward (1958–60) and the Cultural Revolution (1966–72).

into life"[8] is simply a matter of writing about the dark side of society, to the exclusion of heroes or progressive characters. This is a misunderstanding. In varying times and under varying historical circumstances, progressive people must confront varying social problems. A writer cannot portray life separately from actual society, even if he limits his heroes to model workers and war heroes. A writer cannot avoid taking a stance on the great social questions of the day. The several heroic characters that Ru Zhijuan and Liu Zhen have created in the two stories just mentioned are all assertive and courageous in protecting the interests of the masses—which are the same as the interests of socialism—and they all meet with some temporary setbacks. These heroes, who are genuinely part of the tide of history, have won the power to survive; the heroes in those other [overly romantic] literary works have by now lost this power.

Third, literature is a mirror. When the mirror shows us things in life that are not very pretty, or that fall short of our ideals, it is wrong to blame the mirror. Instead we should root out and destroy those conditions that disappoint us. Mirrors show us the true appearance of things; literary mirrors speed the progress of society. Smashing a mirror is no way to make an ugly person beautiful, nor is it a way to make social problems evaporate. History has shown that it is better not to veil or to smash literary mirrors. Isn't this truth all too clear from the extended period of time in which our realist tradition in literature was dragged toward an evil dead end? To forbid literature from delving into life, to deprive writers of their right to reflect on the problems of real life, and not to allow writers to speak for the people harms not only literature but the people and the Party as well. The period of literary history in which such things could happen has now come to an end, and a new chapter has begun. We hope no one will be pulling literature backward any more.

---

8. The phrase "delve into life" (*ganyu shenghuo*) stands for a principle that Liu Binyan adopted in the 1950s from his friend and mentor the Soviet writer Valentin Ovechkin. The principle is that a writer should investigate life for himself and tell the truth, both the good and the bad, about social issues. "Delving into life" has been opposed, in both the Soviet Union and China, by literary officials who prefer that only the rosy side be published.

2. Answer the People's Questions

Our differing views on literary issues have always been bound up with our differing views on politics. And these two kinds of differing views have always derived from the question of how to interpret society and reality.

For example, as some comrades see it, Lin Biao and the Gang of Four did not actually wreak much havoc, and in fact there was no "ultra-leftist line." Others feel that the havoc and the criminal line of the Gang of Four have followed them into collapse and final extinction, and that the only problem remaining today is to get everybody to be productive together.

My view is that the tragedies brought on us by the Gang of Four have yet to be fully exposed, and that what has been exposed is yet to be fully comprehended. The Gang's "residual perniciousness"[9] must not be conceived as something lifeless or static—something just standing by, waiting to be swept away. It is a living social force, and it has its social base.

The perniciousness most worthy of our attention is the invisible kind. The Gang of Four has disrupted the organic workings of our Party and has damaged our social relations. They have created a highly abnormal relationship between our Party and the masses. What makes this matter so difficult to deal with is that many people, while not bad people themselves, either knowingly or unknowingly have been protecting bad people. Superficially they are all Communist Party members or Party cadres; but every action they take serves only their vested interests and comes only from their own habits of thought. This is the very problem I have pointed out in "People or Monsters?" It is not going to go away unless we deal decisively and finally with it.

At this point I would like to bring something to the attention of those comrades who feel that the primary duty of literature is to portray heroes. We are faced today with the ironic fact that heroes are in an awkward position. To do good deeds one has to offend people. One has to take risks and even make a bad name for oneself. When I did newspaper work in the 1950s I always found it hard to initiate criticism of a person. Now, in the late 1970s, I sud-

---

9. *Liudu*, literally "coursing poison," was a standard and politically approved term for the Gang of Four's legacy in 1979.

denly find it has become hard to praise a person. Take, for example, the case of Liu Jie, an inspector of the neighborhood registry in the Daxing'anling district of Heilongjiang, who was praised in the press for sticking to principles. She also had the support of the provincial Party committee. But it was precisely the commendation of the Party newspaper that brought calamity upon her, and the support of the provincial leadership was of no use in breaking the siege that befell her. There were even threats on her life. Now, if a true writer of the people were to interview this progressive young woman, there can be no doubt that he would soon find himself taking sides with her. He would join the battle against wickedness and help her to win a more advantageous position. Only then would he turn to writing up her story. I feel strongly that only this kind of writer deserves the name "writer of the people."

To another group of comrades, those writers and critics who hold that it is the responsibility of literature to introduce modernization and construction, I would like to offer a different observation. The modernization of industry and agriculture is by no means simply a matter of adding new machinery. Human beings are still the mainstay of all productive forces, and the enthusiasm of people today still suffers many artificial constraints. This question deserves notice and additional study.

Methods of enterprise management that are modeled after the patriarchal family system, or after medieval practices or the ways of Genghis Khan, cannot possibly sustain a lasting rise in production. Militaristic methods and political incentives can, it is true, motivate workers over the short term; but as time wears on this approach is also doomed to failure. It is simply incompatible with the nature of modern industry. In history, the birth and development of modern industry has gone hand in hand with the liberation of human beings. This was a qualified liberation, of course. It grew out of the feudal serf system, in which people were bound in their social places. It gave to individuals freedom of their persons as well as certain political rights and legal guarantees of equality. As the individual came to feel that he was an independent person, a free person, a person with a certain dignity and worth, a person equal with others before the law, gradually the ideas "personal character" and "individuality" came into being. Only when the individual attained this kind of status and this kind of consciousness did he begin to rely on himself and devote his talents to the improvement of his lot. The result was that productive forces in the period of capitalism exceeded those of the feudal period many times over. For socialism to exceed capitalism in productivity, it can and must provide even better conditions for human development and advancement. Management principles modeled on the feudal patriarchal system are a step backward from capitalism; they constrict people, inhibit them, and block their abilities and potential. It should go without saying that socialist modernization gains nothing from this.

It may seem that what I've been talking about falls into the realm of economics, but this is not the case. All this has to do with people, and therefore with literature. There are only two ways in which the feudal patriarchal style of leadership supports and extends itself. One is by coercion and command, and the other is by attack and retaliation. And both these methods, because they have, in contemporary political life, become common ways in which a minority can subdue the masses, warrant our closest vigilance. "Power corrupts, and absolute power corrupts absolutely." Without the supervision of the people, a good person will turn bad, and an honest official will turn corrupt.

We must answer the people's questions. We have no right to be auditors in the courtroom of history. The people are the judges, as well as the plaintiffs. We must help supply them with scripts. But before we provide answers, we first must learn. We must understand more about social life than the average person does.

One serious problem is that we still lack an accurate understanding of our own society. Our efforts to understand it have been suspended for many years. In recent times we have not had any sociology, political science, or legal or ethical studies worthy of the name "science." The kind of investigative research that Chairman Mao used to advocate has also been shelved for many years. A vast unknown world lies before us. Consider a few examples.

First, "class struggle." Everyone accepts that class struggle has "expanded" for many years, but in fact, for a long period of time, the target of class struggle was completely misconceived. Its content and methods were also wrong. (In fact, it has been a distinguishing feature of our current historical period that mistakes continually repeat themselves.) Recently a new question has been raised: do classes really exist in our society? Some say they do not. Some say of course they do—just look at Wang Shouxin.[10] Her case shows that after more than twenty years of "struggle," we still haven't figured out whom we ought to be struggling against.

Second, we have worked for more than twenty years at "socialist construction." Yet innumerable problems have dragged on without resolution, and in fact have gotten worse over time. This year our economists have identified the crux of the matter by raising the question of the goals of production under socialism: are we, in the final analysis, producing steel for the sake of steel, and petroleum for the sake of petroleum, or are these things for the people, aimed at satisfying their ever-increasing material and spiritual needs? It seems there are some individuals who do not agree that the goal of production should be to maximize satisfaction of the constantly increasing material and cultural needs of society as a whole.

Third, for many years now we have assigned top priority to "the human factor" in an unending political and ideological revolution. But after many years of this, people's enthusiasm not only has not increased—it has actually declined. This is another question to ponder. It is mystifying that this piece of land called China, always so inhospitable to the cultivation of "rightist opportunism," has nonetheless allowed revisionism with a "leftist" tag to grow so wild.

3. On "People or Monsters?" and Other Things

Our readers need literature with many different themes and styles. But they especially need writers who will serve as spokesmen for the people, writers who will answer their questions and express their demands by confronting the major issues of the day. The welcome for such writers is clearly evident in the spirited applause that plays like "Harbinger of Spring" and "Power Versus Law"[11] have received, and in the wide readership that "People or Monsters?" has had. Some readers worry that "People or Monsters?", which exposes such mas-

---

10. The mastermind of massive embezzlement in "People or Monsters?".

11. "Harbinger of Spring" (Baochun hua) by Cui Dezhi appears in *Drama* (Juben) no. 4, 1979. Set in a factory shortly after the fall of the Gang of Four, it explores a controversy over whether an outstanding employee can be named a "model worker" despite her bad, i.e., bourgeois, class background. "Power Versus Law" (Quan yu fa) by Xing Yixun appears in *Drama* (Juben) no. 10, 1979, and is translated in *Chinese Literature* (Beijing), June 1980. The play criticizes officials who abuse power for selfish purposes.

sive problems, creates a negative or pessimistic mood in readers, causing them to lose faith in our Party and our system. I have received a great number of thought-provoking letters from readers of "People or Monsters?", and judging from these, there is no such danger. The reader response is positive. The work triggers a burst of righteousness in people; it arouses the ardent wish of everyone who cares about our country to cure our illness and save our society. Some readers have even gone to Chairman Hua[12] with concrete proposals for reform. But the opposition to "People or Monsters?" of course has been fierce, too. I have awoken to a hard fact: in today's China, if one speaks or writes and does not incur somebody's opposition, one might as well not have spoken or written at all. One has no alternative. The only alternative is to cower in a corner and fall silent. But if we do that, why live?

We are writing in the particular time and circumstances of China at the juncture between the 1970s and the 1980s. The needs of the times and the demands of the people must be our commands. Our role is necessitated by the inexorable development of history. We have no right to sidestep the immensely complex problems of our society. We must help our readers to understand our society more profoundly and accurately, and help them to rise in struggle for the complete realization of the great historical task of the Four Modernizations![13]

---

12. Hua Guofeng (b. 1921) was Chairman of the Communist Party of China from October 24, 1976, until June 29, 1981.

13. "The Four Modernizations" is a program to modernize industry, agriculture, national defense, and science and technology by the year 2000. First enunciated by Zhou Enlai at the Fourth People's Congress (January 13–17, 1975), the plan became the dominant policy of the Deng Xiaoping regime in the late 1970s.

PEOPLE OR MONSTERS?

TRANSLATED BY JAMES V. FEINERMAN,
WITH PERRY LINK

"Reportage" (baogaowenxue) *is a modern Chinese genre that falls between literary art and news report. Good reportage differs from ordinary news reporting in several ways: it is longer and more carefully written, and while it may begin from an event in the news, its author seeks to uncover aspects of the social background that are more basic and enduring than the news event itself.*

"People or Monsters?" is reportage and cannot be properly appreciated unless viewed that way. The story of Wang Shouxin's massive corruption in Bin County, Heilongjiang Province, was widely known in China before Liu Binyan ever went there to do his investigation. Hence he does not bother, for example, to introduce his characters in ways that are conventional for Chinese fiction. His contribution—and it is a formidable one, given the barriers and risks involved—was patiently to gather and check facts, and then to piece them together into a single mosaic whose unity lies not only in the logical coherence of the whole, but also in the steady moral presence of the author. He could easily have treated Wang Shouxin as a scapegoat, as so many others were treating the Gang of Four; instead, he has coolly analyzed the basic social conditions that had allowed her corruption to grow. When these conditions were documented and published, readers everywhere in China recognized them, to a greater or lesser degree, in their own environments. It is this fact that made "People or Monsters?" so widely popular, and also this fact that brought the wrath of certain political critics upon Liu Binyan. The reaction in Heilongjiang Province, where some of the characters in "People or Monsters?" were still in power, was particularly intense. Some even charged that Liu Binyan had written the piece in order to make a fortune by selling it to Americans.[1]

We must not overlook the importance to contemporary Chinese writers and readers of the simple truth-stating function of literature. To do so can lead us

Originally published in *Renmin wenxue* (Beijing), no. 9, 1979.
1. *Wenyi qingkuang*, no. 9 (1980): 13–15.

toward literary judgments of a piece like "People or Monsters?" that are beside
the point. For example, when Liu Binyan documents corruption at some
length and does not cover the fact that the Communist Party itself is com-
plexly involved in it, he sometimes appears to condescend to his readers with
brusque "authorial intrusions," such as the famous line "The Communist
Party regulated everything, but would not regulate the Communist Party."
But it is wrong to say that readers are here receiving a simple-minded sum-
mary, or that the author arrogantly supposes that they need one; the point for
readers—which was exhilarating—was that here, finally, in print, with the
prestige of publication in People's Literature *and the moral authority of a*
writer who was famous for his conscience and his courage, was a statement
that many had had in mind but never dared, save in the most secure
confidence, to utter. Writers like Liu Binyan know and respect their readers'
feelings. What they are doing by putting their punch lines in black and white
is the very opposite of condescension.

  In October 1979, Liu Binyan spoke out in defense of the student literary
journal Our Generation *just before this "unofficial publication" was shut*
down by the authorities. In January 1980, Liu published "Warning," which
was subsequently declared to betray "a lack of faith in Party central." Under
increasing pressure, Liu wrote a letter to the Central Propaganda Department
in spring 1980, in which he set the record straight on some rumors about him,
but also apologized to the Party. "I've always had the problem of being
insufficiently serious," he wrote, "and I have said some inappropriate things. I
have also allowed my biases to emerge. . . ."[2] In the months following delivery
of this letter the political pressure on Liu Binyan seems to have abated; cer-
tainly it was much lower by fall of 1982, when Liu was given permission,
after earlier denials, to accept a long-standing invitation to the International
Writers' Workshop at the University of Iowa.—ED.

The courtyard of the Party Committee of Bin County had long been
the center of attention for the people of the entire county. During the
ten years following land reform, people constantly came and went, as
casually as if they were dropping in on their relatives. Whatever
problem or circumstance brought you to the town market, or some-
where else in town, you could always go to the county hall to pass the
time for a while, chatting with the cadres who were in charge of that
year's work teams in your village. After a time, however, the courtyard walls seemed to grow slowly taller and thicker, so that when
commoners passed by, or popped in for a look, they felt somewhat
afraid, somewhat awed by the mysteriousness within. By the early

---

2. Ibid., pp. 13–15.

1960s, when people who hurried past the courtyard's main gate could smell enticing odors of meat, cooking oil, and steamed bread, they felt that something wasn't quite right. Their mouths would contort into bitter smiles. Being an official isn't bad at all, they would think to themselves.

In November 1964, a crowd of people gathered at the gate of the courtyard, where a jeep had just driven in. The people had heard that a new Party secretary was coming, and they wanted to see for themselves what kind of person he would be. Their intense curiosity was mixed with eager anticipation, and not a little worry, too: the present County Party Committee had run through three secretaries already—would the new one be able to make it?

From the moment he arrived, Tian Fengshan, a tall, ruddy-cheeked outlander, became the object of everyone's attention. Before long people began to say, "*His* Communist Party and theirs are quite different."

At that time, Bin County in Heilongjiang Province had just begun recovering from the three years of economic hardship.[3] The people had paid a great price for these years, and there were quite a few problems that now required the serious consideration and reappraisal of the Party Committee. Yet at the meetings of the Standing Committee of the County Party Committee, and at the study classes for Party members at Two Dragon Mountain, all the talk was about women. . . .

Tian Fengshan was taking over from a rotten bunch of leaders. While the people were living off tree bark and leaves, making food from a "flour" of crumbled corncobs and cornstalks, the children of the County Party secretary were amusing themselves by tossing meat-filled dumplings made with fine white flour at dogs in the street. Peasants, carrying small packs of dried grain with them, would trek more than thirty miles to present petitions to the County Party Committee, only to be met with icy stares. This is why people seldom approached the County Party Committee any more; those with problems went straight to the provincial capital at Harbin. And so it came about that the County Party secretary and members of the

---

3. Bad harvests in 1959, 1960, and 1961 were the results of natural calamities in addition to man-made calamities caused by the policies of the Great Leap Forward, a highly impractical effort to get instant results in industry and agriculture.

Standing Committee had even more time to relax in their armchairs and discuss their favorite topic.

Tian Fengshan began personally receiving petitions from the masses and he personally took care of ten important unjust cases that had dragged on for many years. People would begin arriving at his door before he had even got out of bed. He would chew on dried grain as he listened to their complaints. He also went around to all the restaurants and stores in the county seat checking the quality of their goods and services. He rescinded the title "Advanced Enterprise" that had been given regularly each year to the food products factory. "True, you earn tens of thousands of dollars[4] each year," he told them, "and true, you save tens of thousands of pounds of rice, oil and sugar. But you do this by cheating the common people—what kind of 'advanced enterprise' is that?" Having inquired into housing conditions, he lowered rents. He brought cadres to see the more backward production brigades, and immediately the poorer brigades began to change for the better.

But history allotted him a mere two years! In November 1966, Red Guards stormed the courtyard of the County Party Committee. Within two hours the man who had been honored by the people of Bin County as "Honest Magistrate Tian" retired forever from the stage of Bin County's history.

As the lonely, looming figure of Tian Fengshan fell into obscurity, a new star began to rise in the Bin County seat. This fellow was thin and small and quite ordinary in appearance; but because of his military rank he quickly became all-powerful, a great figure who held sway over the 500,000 people in Bin County. Even today, thirteen years later, the political achievements of this leftist Commissar Yang are felt in the daily lives of the people of Bin County; people often think about him and discuss him, always sharply contrasting him with their fond memories of Tian Fengshan.

The first impressions Commissar Yang left with people were of his quacking voice and his inflammatory public speeches. Yet while people were still sorting out these first impressions, one thing had already aroused everybody's interest. Whenever Commissar Yang's jeep drove by on the dirt road from the county seat, raising a cloud of

4. Here and throughout this book, "dollars" refers to the equivalent of 1979 U.S. dollars. Measures of length, area, weight, etc. are converted to miles, acres, tons, etc.

dust, people felt puzzled: "Why was Commissar Yang running around with that woman?"

The woman with Commissar Yang in the car was shortly to become an important figure in Bin County and would, thirteen years later, shock the entire country. She was Wang Shouxin.

Enter "Leftist" Wang Shouxin

On the eve of the storm, things were just a little too quiet at the tiny Bin County Coal Company. Party Branch Secretary Bai Kun and Manager Teng Zhixin, both from poor peasant backgrounds, had been keeping this little enterprise of a few dozen workers in apple-pie order. The spirit of the time was to learn from the heroic soldier Lei Feng; cadres were honest and labored for the public good. Yet peering back through the murky clouds of the past thirteen years, it probably cannot be said that there were no problems at the coal company. For example, Zhou Lu, the person who had been nominated by the Party to succeed the Party branch secretary that year (we here pass over the question of whether it was right to designate this person in advance, since Party secretaries are supposed to be elected), later became an accomplice in Wang Shouxin's massive corruption scheme. By contrast, Liu Changchun, one who was reckoned at that time to be ideologically backward, later fought tirelessly against Wang Shouxin, and never did yield to her.

Wang Shouxin began as the company's cashier. She was full of energy, but unfortunately all of it was directed outside the company. One moment she would be sitting there and the next—whee!—she had disappeared. She was always first to find out who had been fighting with whom in public, which couple was headed for divorce, or what new goods had just arrived at the department store. She always took it upon herself to spread around whatever she could learn, and her old-biddy gossiping often set her comrades against one another.

When the great billows of the Cultural Revolution rolled along, they stimulated God knows which ones of Wang Shouxin's animal desires, but in any case brought out in her political urges that had lain dormant for many years. At first she tried to establish herself in commercial circles, but no one would have her. She tried the students, but had no luck there either. She finally got some support when she reached Commissar Yang of the Munitions Ministry; then she returned to the coal company and tried to build an organization. When no one would cooperate, she went after Zhang Feng, who was a former bandit. "Let's team up," she said. "Let's bash them to smithereens! We'll call ourselves the 'Smash-the-Black-Nest Combat Force'!"

She also drew aside the driver Zhou Lu, a Party member, and prodded him gently in the ribs with her elbow. "You've been oppressed, too," she wheedled, eyebrows prancing and eyeballs dancing. "Why don't you seize the time and rebel?"

This person Zhou Lu was, unfortunately, afraid of his own shadow, despite his huge frame. He was afraid that rebellion could lead to misfortune. Yet if he didn't rebel, but just watched as Wang Shouxin became the trusted lackey of Commissar Yang, he feared even worse consequences. He thought long and hard, and finally decided that the old bunch of officeholders like Bai Kun would never return. Bucking up his courage, he climbed aboard Wang Shouxin's bandwagon. Wang had often taunted him: "Marry a hawk and eat meat; marry a duck and eat chickenshit." Zhou Lu finally made up his mind that he had to have meat.

The first person obstructing Wang Shouxin's way was Liu Changchun. This man had been a handicraft worker, a weaver; now he was the planner and accountant for the coal company. His dependents included five of his siblings in addition to his wife and children, and he could hardly stretch his salary to support all of them. After a long day's work, when others were going home to relax or going out to amuse themselves, Liu Changchun had to moonlight. He made use of his weaving skill by mending socks, and he sometimes sold beansprouts in the market. He would earn scarcely a couple of dimes for one night's work. He tried occasionally to raise a piglet that he would buy at the market; but he didn't know how to feed piglets and could even end up losing money when he sold them. In sum, he refused to join in all the framing and the fawning, the stealing and the sneaking. He just carried on, repeatedly managing to muster energy from his thin and withered frame, never bemoaning his sorry lot. He wouldn't curse the fates for not favoring him, or turn into a sourpuss; and he seemed always able to keep his spirits up.

Probably because of his suffering as a child, or perhaps because of the obstinate disposition that is typical in craftsmen, Liu Changchun would not bow and scrape or put up with scurrilous talk. He would stick his neck out, glare with a pair of eyes that took no account of the reaction of the person glared at, and say things that offended people. Moreover, in order to take care of his family, he had to spend time every day on his "private plot," and this, in the eyes of the Party leadership, removed him even further from favor.

Wang Shouxin's "Smash-the-Black-Nest Combat Force" challenged Liu Changchun's "Red Rebel Corps" to a debate.

Liu Changchun could not conceive of Wang Shouxin as a serious adversary. But he was viewing her only as an individual and failed to see the influence that she had already accumulated. At the outset he had committed the mistake of underestimating his enemy.

At the public debate that followed, a short, thin fellow took the platform. Hands behind his back, he squared his shoulders and puffed up his chest. At first Liu Changchun was dismayed, thinking him to be some leader from Harbin. But when he looked more closely he burst out laughing: "It's only *that* little bastard. He's been the rebel leader only three days, and he's already trying to act the part."

The man was Wen Feng, director of the "United Program to Defend Mao Zedong Thought." He was coming out in support of Wang Shouxin, and he didn't have to say very much. It was enough that he flap his lips a few times, using his deep voice and clear enunciation to show off for a moment his long-dormant ability as a public speaker. Most important was the slogan that he tacked on at the end to intimidate everyone. "Follow Commissar Yang closely," he said. "Resolutely make revolution; sweep away all ghosts and monsters!"

Commissar Yang was standing next to Wen Feng and Wang Shouxin. One's attitude toward Yang had become the new acid test that separated revolutionary from counterrevolutionary.

Up on stage, Wang Shouxin was wearing her shiny black hair cut short and pulled back behind her ears. Although she had been wearing less makeup since her decision to become a rebel, her fair-skinned face appeared lively and pretty, making her look younger than her forty-five years.

Commissar Yang had specially deputed an officer of his to take charge of the debate. The deputy's word was law on every question. "Liu Changchun," he pronounced, "your Red Rebel Corps has allowed the powerholders to get away with things: you let them stress production and suppress revolution. You still go to them to 'study the problems of production.' Where do you show the slightest bit of rebel spirit? Your group is rightist! Your whole direction is wrong! You are ordered to disband beginning today!"

Liu Changchun was furious. This was absurd! Convicted before he even had a chance to say anything! Liu had always liked to read newspapers and think for himself. He was proud of his ability to understand policies and to address them. Now he scrambled onto the platform clutching the "Sixteen Points" and the "latest directives"; clearing his throat and assuming a bold stance, he was all set to tie into them. He was too naïve to realize that the scriptures he possessed were already out-of-date. He was met by a deafening uproar of slogans; then he was jostled, and there was punching and kicking as well. This special modern form of "debate" used in our ancient, civilized country is most efficient. Within two minutes Wang Shouxin's political enemy had been "refuted" beyond any hope of recovery.

Any number of struggle sessions were held, but Liu Changchun refused to bow his head. Once when his head was physically pressed down, he still laughed and looked around the room, as if seeking someone to share his joke or hear his sarcastic comment. Zhou Lu, who was in charge of this session, shouted himself hoarse, only to find Liu Changchun still fighting to raise his head and answer back. "Hey, Zhou Lu, you really are a goddamn bumpkin! Why do you have to shout your pisser voicebox dry?"

This comment put Zhou Lu on the spot, and greatly amused all who heard it.

The day after the debate, when Wang Shouxin had seen there was no one around but the two of them, she stole up to Liu Changchun and whispered into his ear: "Let's work together, Changchun. I am not very literate, and I need you as my military adviser. I'll be in charge, and you can be number two . . ."

Liu Changchun's eyes widened. "You can knock that off right now!" he replied in a voice as hard as nails. "I'd rather be the stable boy of a gentleman than the ancestor of a bastard! You'll get yours—just wait!"

That was precisely his style—refusing to give in even when he was butting his head against a stone wall. Most other people had already gone over to Wang Shouxin, and her influence was growing greater and greater. Meanwhile the Red Rebel Corps was falling apart. Yet

Liu Changchun tried to rally the spirits of those in his faction who had still not fought back. "Don't worry," he said, "if you land in jail I'll bring you your meals."

He never imagined that, within a few days, he himself would be taken off to jail in handcuffs, charged as an "anti-Army" active counterrevolutionary.

The World Turned Upside Down

In poor and backward areas the fragrance of the flower of political power has its greatest allure. Were this not so, the "rebel" leader Wen Feng could never have been up front shouting, "Follow Commissar Yang closely," nor could he ever have benefited from doing so. To be perfectly fair, when Commissar Yang first heard the slogan he was taken aback and asked someone around him, "What's he saying?" The person who was asked had been clever enough to reply, "Weren't you sent here from Chairman Mao's headquarters? Of course we must follow you closely!" Commissar Yang then assented. "Yes, yes," he said, nodding his head. "You should follow me closely."

Close behind "following closely" came loving and adoring. One day when he came to the office, Commissar Yang found he had left his keys at home; without saying a word, his female secretary immediately hopped onto a bus to fetch the keys. Separately and simultaneously, his driver showed up at his home too. Each was hiding his motives from the other in order to be the one to return the keys. After arguing each other to a standstill, they finally agreed to bring them to the commissar together and share the praise.

In brief, the force of Commissar Yang's prestige in Bin County was the same as the force of the potential of bullets to kill people. When Wang Shouxin accompanied Commissar Yang on an inspection tour of a commune late one night and informed the commune cadres that "Commissar Yang's favorite dish is boiled meat with pickled cabbage and blood sausage, but the meat must be lean," it was obvious that she was savoring the taste of real power, and that she liked this taste at least as much as that of the famous Manchurian dish.

One day in August 1968, Commissar Yang strode briskly and boldly into the planning office of the Bin County Commercial Revolutionary Committee. He looked around the room at the committee members, all of whom had risen out of respect. Then, in his customarily firm voice, he shocked everyone by saying, "Wang Shouxin must be allowed to join you on this committee."

The committee members all looked at one another without a word. At last one of them courageously asked, in a low voice, "If she joined, what could she contribute?" What he meant was that she couldn't read a character the size of the big dipper. Then there was her reputation . . . for sleeping around . . .

Commissar Yang was pacing around the office, as though lost in thought. When he heard this objection he stopped short and glared fiercely at the officials before him. He knit his brows and then spoke irritably, in words as clear and immutable as boldface type: "The question is not whether she should join, but whether she should be the vice-chair!"

This was an order, and as such as it was adopted immediately and unanimously by the committee, who did not bother to wait for a referendum among the commercial workers of Bin County. For those days, this was normal. If it hadn't been, why would Commissar Yang have had to knit his brows? That scowl admits several interpretations: "You hopeless boneheads!", or "What's this? You people are anti-Army?" or "Maybe you didn't mean it when you all shouted 'Follow closely'!"

Actually Commissar Yang had worries of his own. Wang Shouxin had been begging him for a position since 1967, insisting that she be made head of the Women's Congress. This puzzled the highest authorities. She wasn't even a Party Committee member, so how could she be the head? Impossible. Wang Shouxin was greatly put out. She had "rebelled"; she had been running around with Commissar Yang; she had, for the first time in her life, come to enjoy the taste of power in this society of ours. So many people obeying a single voice, playing up to you, flattering you! What power! What fame! How much more honorable this was than her former ideal—to be the wife of a collaborationist policeman or a landlord.

But now she had become deeply disappointed, and went around complaining about Commissar Yang behind his back. "Commissar Yang, my eye! He's less than a prick hair! And those bitches at the Women's Congress are all sluts!"

After that Commissar Yang again ordered the Commercial Revolutionary Committee to "receive" Wang Shouxin into the Party. A number of members opposed her; even the Commercial Committee chairman, Zhao Yu, who had resolutely opposed and smashed Tian Fengshan (in those days, the degree to which one opposed Tian Fengshan separated "revolutionary" from "nonrevolutionary" and "counterrevolutionary"), found it hard to "follow Commissar Yang closely." Hence the entire committee bore the brunt of the commissar's wrath: "Still needs training? Will you kindly tell me in what way she needs training? Isn't the Great Cultural Revolution the test of a person? As far as I can see, she's the only person in Bin County fit to enter the Party!"

A month later, in an address to the Workers' Congress, Commissar Yang told more than five hundred people that "some people still have misgivings about the rebels. They find minor faults, but fail to see the big picture. Here are all these rebels and no one seeks to cultivate them. Instead, you cultivate easy-going types for entrance to the Party." In the end, despite the opposition of 70 percent of the Party members, Wang Shouxin joined the Party as a member "specially endorsed" by Commissar Yang.

This happened in September of 1969. In the very same month, a fine Party member named Zhang Zhixin was arrested in Liaoning Province by a dictatorship organ of the Communist Party.[5] One had joined and one had been kicked out. Tian Fengshan had fallen and Commissar Yang had risen. Were these merely insignificant accidents in their implications for communist organization in China?

Ten years had to pass before anyone could even raise questions about this massive inversion of justice.

Wonderful Exchange

On the day that Wang Shouxin first took over as manager and Party secretary of the coal company (which was later called the fuel company), some workers were digging trenches for oil pipes. Some members of the county work team were playing chess in the office. When she saw this Wang Shouxin flared up. "Well I'll be damned," she yelled. "You play chess while others work. What kind of work team is this?"

Zhou Lu, now the assistant manager, was shocked; Wang Shouxin

---

5. A campaign was under way in 1979 to praise the young woman Zhang Zhixin, who spoke out against repression during the Cultural Revolution and paid for it with her life.

had never yelled at anyone like that before. What he didn't realize was that someone at that very moment was observing *him,* and that this person was also shocked by certain changes. The observer was the old Party secretary at the coal company, Bai Kun, and there was something he couldn't figure out: this guy Zhou Lu had never been very good at his job—once when he was driving a car he had lost a wheel and didn't even notice it. That I can forgive, mused Bai Kun, but—though I always thought highly of his character and even felt I could train him to take over for me—suddenly he appears to have changed entirely. He fawns over Wang Shouxin like crazy, patting the woman's ass whenever she speaks. It must have been the same, all this flattering and fawning, when he worked for me. But because it made me feel comfortable, I always felt it was a virtue. How could I have failed to see through him all these years?

There were many things that had not been seen through. Just look at Wang Shouxin—she too had seemed to change completely. Formerly she had been lazy and useless, but now she was the first one on the job and the last to leave. Even her clothing changed drastically— she wore a cotton jacket and rubber shoes. All day long she would be running in and out of the office, busy as a bee, laboring along with the workers who were unloading coal or cleaning up.

Over the years Wang Shouxin had come to know this tiny coal company thoroughly, and to become thoroughly bored with it. Yet once she became boss, all that changed; everything now seemed to take on a strange radiance. Jet black coal piles, glistening lumps of coal—how delightful! No longer was she bored with those who were busy unloading the coal, weighing it or collecting payment for it. Everything now belonged to her, and everybody obeyed Wang Shouxin's orders.

Of course Wang Shouxin supposed that she was "serving the people." But "the people" were various: they differed in quality and rank. The first reform she carried out was to sell coal according to a person's position. She arranged to have the top-grade coal picked out and packed in waterproof straw bags for delivery by truck directly to the doors of the County Party secretary and the members of the Standing Committee. This was coal that caught fire quickly and burned well—just right for cooking dumplings at New Year's. And payment? "What's the rush? We'll discuss it later . . . "

As for the people's armed forces, no question about it—nothing was nearer and dearer to Wang Shouxin's heart than the brown padded coats of the military. Soldiers were on the top rung of her class ladder. Right below them came the Organization Department. These people were sent the best grade of coal, delivered in special trucks, and were treated to meals to boot. Next in line were those concerned with personnel, finance, and labor.

Wang Shouxin was a warmly sentimental woman with clearly defined likes and dislikes. Her tens of thousands of tons of coal and her nine trucks were the brush and ink that she used every day to compose her lyric poems.

The distilleries and provisions factories produced the sweet, enticing smells of famous liquors, pastries, and candies. Wang Shouxin was not a glutton; no, what she sought from these sweet smells was only the smiling faces of provincial-, prefectural-, and county-level "connections." For this reason, such factories could rely on a never-ending supply of fine-quality coal at low prices. Wang Shouxin couldn't care less about the bearings factory or the porcelain factories. These produced nothing but cold, hard little knickknacks. Who would ever want gifts like that? So these factories got low-grade coal, with prices jacked up at that. What if a factory was losing money? Going bankrupt? What if the coal could not burn hot enough to heat large vats? None of *that* had anything to do with the great Wang Shouxin!

One year in January the county hospital ran out of coal. A man was sent to seek out Manager Wang. After looking over his letter of introduction, Wang Shouxin raised her eyebrows and questioned the man. "How come your top man didn't come?"

"He's busy, he didn't have time . . ."

"A man named Gao Dianyou from your hospital has informed against my son. No coal for you!"

The man begged and pleaded, but Wang Shouxin wouldn't give an inch. "Your Gao Dianyou accused my son of adultery," she continued. "The County Party Committee has been investigating for two months already, and my son is still the vice-director of the Xinli Commune, isn't he? Don't think you can slip one past Old Lady Wang! This exposé of my son is the work of Fang Yongjiu of Xinli Commune and was prepared by Director Rong of the Commune's Health Department. Gao Dianyou is just their mouthpiece!"

When word got back to Gao Dianyou, he immediately wrote a letter to the County Party Committee: ". . . There is obviously something fishy going on here. How could Wang Shouxin know so much about my exposé of Liu Zhimin? I request the County Committee to give this matter their closest attention and to take measures to assure my physical safety."

This was not the first time, nor would it be the last, that an accusation against Wang Shouxin fell into the hands of Wang Shouxin. It was also not the first or last time that Wang Shouxin brazenly used the coal she controlled as a weapon for revenge.

Trucks were also important instruments in Wang Shouxin's system of rewards and revenge. Every fall people in Bin County had to go up to the mountains for firewood and down to the villages for vegetables in order to get through the winter. And in a county seat with a population of 30,000, trucks were hard to come by. Yet this was an ordeal every family had to undergo every year.

Inspector Yang Qing of the County Inspectorate had that year asked a driver to go to the mountains for firewood. His family prepared a complete banquet for the returning driver—no mean feat on a salary of about thirty dollars a month. When it was almost dark, they could hear the truck returning, and the whole family rushed out for a look. The truck had come back empty! The driver's face revealed his displeasure. "Roads were blocked," he said, and drove his truck back home. How would this family get through the winter? They were on the verge of tears. Husband and wife looked helplessly at the banquet spread, which was getting colder and colder.

Then in their hour of despair, who was it that lent them a helping hand?—Old Lady Wang. How could the whole family not be grateful?

Wang Shouxin was deeply concerned about the difficulties of people in Bin County. The county cadres' wages hadn't risen for over ten years, and every family felt the pinch. Many had borrowed anywhere from several hundred to nearly a thousand dollars of public funds. In 1975 the County Committee, on instructions from above, insisted on a deadline for the return of the public funds. Enter Wang Shouxin, the "goddess of wealth." She always carried with her a passbook for an unregistered bank account, and she could produce ready cash just by reaching into the drawer of her office desk.

People she could use didn't even have to open their mouths; Wang Shouxin would approach *them*: "Having problems? Short of cash?"

The rebel leader Wen Feng and his pals, as well as the leaders of many important offices, all "borrowed" public funds that Wang Shouxin had appropriated without the niceties of bookkeeping, and then used that money to repay their own debts to the public. A new relationship arose from this transfer of the proletarian state's money: first, Wang Shouxin, rather than the state, assumed the creditor's role; second, Wang Shouxin's money did not necessarily have to be returned. In fact, she preferred that it not be returned, because then people would owe her their loyalty and future favors. But even if the money was returned, the debts of favor would remain. The favorite method of repaying these obligations was for the debtor to use his own power for Wang Shouxin's convenience. This caused the debtor no material loss, and for Wang Shouxin it was more than she could buy for a thousand pieces of gold. So why not do it this way, since it had such benefits for both sides?

At bottom, all this was an exchange of goods that was effected by trading off power. One form of this barter involved the direct handling of goods. For example, Wang Shouxin raised a large number of pigs, pork being another item in her power-brokering. But where could she get fodder for the pigs? Just seek out the vice-director of the Grain Bureau, of course! More than five tons of corn, bran, soybeans, and husks were sent right over. Later on, Wang Shouxin needed flour, rice, and soybean oil for her partying and gift-giving. No problem! Just call the vice-director again! And thus it happened that, in the short span of one year, another five tons of rice, flour, and soybean oil passed into her hands. In return, the vice-director could "borrow" money or bricks from Wang Shouxin, or "buy" complete cartloads of coal on credit. Payment was never required, and in fact no payment was ever made.

In this county, the organs of the "dictatorship of the proletariat" served Wang Shouxin's "socialist" enterprises extremely well. Wang Shouxin would dispatch carts loaded with meat, fish, grain, oil, or vegetables to Harbin, in violation of county regulations. When this happened, the chief of the Section for Industry and Commerce, who was also second-in-command of the "rebels," would give special approval under his own signature. From 1973 on, her vehicles could come and go unhindered. In return, this fellow received a "loan" of four hundred dollars plus a variety of presents. On one occasion Wang Shouxin had to "safeguard" some cash that properly belonged to the central government. She needed it for her private dealings and building, so she couldn't put it in a bank account; that was when the deputy chief of the Finance Section, another of her "rebel" friends, opened account number 83001. To it she diverted hundreds of thousands of dollars, which were always at her disposal in a perfectly legal and protected place. To repay this man, Wang Shouxin arranged to have his son-in-law transferred from the temporary labor force to a permanent job. Then she admitted his son to the "Camp for Educated Youths" she had set up and, after falsifying his credentials, arranged his admission to a university.

For years this trading of influence went on between Wang Shouxin and dozens of officials—perhaps a hundred—on the County Party Committee, County Revolutionary Committee, and at the district and even the provincial levels. Many of these people used their status as the capital for their trade. Once Wang Shouxin, in order to set up a "nonstaple foodstuffs base," needed to take over more than thirty-three acres of good land that belonged to the Pine River Brigade of the Raven River Commune. This infuriated the commune members and local cadres. The head of the County Agricultural Office, who lacked the power to approve this deal, arranged a meal where he brought Wang Shouxin together with the leaders of the commune, the brigade, and the production teams that were involved. This gave the impression that the County Revolutionary Committee supported the discussions and acquiesced in the illegal dealings. Thus a huge tract of arable land changed hands.

This kind of "socialist" exchange does indeed demonstrate great "superiority" over capitalist exchange; neither party has to have any capital of his own, there is no need to put up private possessions as collateral, and no one needs to run any risk of loss or bankruptcy. Everybody gets what he wants.

One thing was completely clear, however. Not a single one of these exchanges could have been made without a departure from Party policy, or without either causing direct loss of socialist public property or breaking Party regulations and national laws. In some cases all of these violations occurred. Eventually, this had to harm the socialist system and discredit the Party's leadership. Through the incessant bartering, Party and government cadres slowly degenerated into parasitical insects that fed off the people's productivity and the socialist system. The relationship between the Party and the masses deteriorated greatly.

How Can a Single Hand Clap?

Language is a strange thing. When Commissar Yang pointed to Wang Shouxin as having a "completely red family," he had meant to praise her. Yet, in the mouths of the common people, the same phrase—"completely red family"—was said as a curse. When they went down the list of Wang Shouxin's family and asked how each had entered the Party or risen to official positions, they rejected all of these relatives one by one.

Her eldest son, Liu Zhimin, was a lazy oaf who could think only of women. He almost always looked half-drunk. What could possibly have qualified him to become a member of the Chinese Communist Party? And how did he become vice-director of Xinli Commune? When he tried to rape a girl, why was it that he was treated with such leniency, and even assigned thereafter to the County Committee "to make policy"? Wang Shouxin's second son entered the Party from a cadre school that had only a temporary branch, one without the power to recruit Party members. And what about her youngest, that totally unqualified young dandy who got appointed assistant manager of the photography studio? Even stranger was Wang Shouxin's younger sister, who, shortly after being expelled from the Communist Youth League, managed to enter the Party! . . .

Since the people loved the Party, they were of course going to be upset when they saw these shady characters sneak into it! From 1972 onwards, any time a political campaign came along, people would flock to the Party Committee to put up big character posters with their questions about Wang Shouxin and her "completely red family."

Yet the Party organization of Bin County could not be reformed until there was a change in the Party leadership. The opportunity for this came in 1970. Early in the year, because of his success in "supporting the Left," Commissar Yang was appointed head of the security task force for all of Heilongjiang Province. He was succeeded as Bin County Party secretary by an old cadre named Zhang Xiangling. Zhang was a solidly built, middle-aged man, with a pair of big, thick-soled feet. In 1945 he had *walked* all the way from Yan'an to Baiquan County in Heilongjiang. Now he was preparing to make use of his big feet again to take the measure of Bin County. Despite a severe stomach ailment, he could cover as many as thirty-five miles in one day.

But he quickly discovered one place where he could hardly take a single step, and that was inside the courtyard of the Party Committee. For Commissar Yang, even after receiving his transfer orders, hung on in Bin County for several months; he had reorganized administrative power so that each important position at the section level and above was filled by a "rebel" member. Most of the regular cadres of Bin County were still down in the countryside or were under house arrest.

Whenever Zhang Xiangling tried to free one of these cadres, the "Cultural Revolution Group" would inform him that they planned to hold a criticism and struggle session concerning that cadre the next day, and they requested Zhang's attendance. The power of the "Cultural Revolution Group" was much like that of the Beijing group of the same name [headed by Mao Zedong and his wife Jiang Qing]; its deputy leader also happened to be a woman—Wang Shouxin's daughter-in-law.

This woman was in her twenties, not very tall but slender and pretty. Her smile disclosed a pair of comely canines that made her even more attractive. As a typist at the County People's Committee she was fine. But once Commissar Yang appointed this poorly educated, minimally capable woman to be deputy head of the Cultural Revolution Group, she suddenly became another person altogether.

Nothing causes self-delusion quite so readily as power. The very day this woman achieved power, she began—mistakenly—to convince herself that she had the education, the moral stature, and the ability that such a position called for. The vanity, narrowness, and jealousy that had lain dormant in the typist's heart were all suddenly awakened. Her lovely eyes now flared with suspicion and hatred, as they followed and searched out her potential enemies. The tears she had shed at the departure of Commissar Yang now changed to enmity for Zhang Xiangling. Whenever a meeting took her to Harbin, she always went to see Commissar Yang, and in this way Bin County remained subject to Yang's will through a kind of remote control.

For a while Zhang Xiangling had only this one power: he could absent himself from criticism and struggle sessions. His situation bore a startling resemblance to the position of Chinese magistrates under the puppet regime of Manchukuo [occupied northeast China, 1932–45], where real power lay in the hands of the Japanese. Yet unlike those days, when there was only one Japanese deputy magistrate, now there were "Japanese" all over the place. The "rebels" who held the deputy positions in each of the sections had greater power than that of the formal section heads.

In order that readers have no misunderstanding, I must do a little explaining about the "rebels" of Bin County. The Bin County high school students who had been "Red Guards" had long ago been quelled by the "Unified Program to Defend Mao Zedong Thought." The Red Guards' crime had been that they were "anti-Army." Those who took over the power also called themselves "Red Guards" at first, and wore red armbands. But actually they were stubble-bearded cadres, many of them well over forty and old enough to be grand-parents. They belonged to the generation of the Red Guards' parents. The important distinction, however, was not that of age. It was primarily that they all had families to feed and were much more interested in economics than the youngsters had been. Second, many of them had "rebelled" because of the frustration of having failed, after many years in officialdom, to enter the Party or to be promoted. These people could think of nothing but their desires for material improvement, political power, and influence.

What worried Zhang Xiangling most was that not only the leader-ship but the whole Party organization was growing more corrupt daily. One married couple who entered the Party in 1969, right after Wang Shouxin had, were overheard fighting with each other in this fashion: "What're you so uppity about? A few bottles of good liquor were your ticket of admission to the Party!"

"Goddamn it, you're worse than I. You think you could have joined without that pretty face of yours?"

Only by doing his utmost, and at the risk of his own Party member-ship, was Zhang Xiangling finally able to remove from office a few of the most detested "rebel" leaders. In 1970 there was a resolution to reinvestigate the pack of rascals who had entered the party in 1969. Yet, when he left Bin County in 1972, Zhang had to admit that he had failed to change the balance of political power in Bin County. Not long thereafter, those he had removed from power came back; his resolution to purge bad elements from the Party was never put into effect.

Zhang Xiangling left behind several newly constructed factories in Bin County. He could hardly have imagined that these factories would lose money year after year and would make little contribution to the central government treasury, but would help line the pockets of grafters, thieves, and powerholders.

"A Heroine of Her Times"

Many differing accounts of Wang Shouxin's character circulated among the people of Bin County. "Old Lady Wang is straightforward; she doesn't hold anything back." "Wang Shouxin is the world's greatest phony, and she's also a bare-faced liar." "Old Lady Wang is good hearted, warm, and concerned about people." "Wang Shouxin is vicious and hounds people to death."

All these descriptions were true. She could be straightforward one moment and phony the next. Two months earlier her heart might have bled for you, but two months later she'd be hounding you. All of this was not incompatible. It may seem so, but we shall gradually see how it all fit together.

When she found a worker crouching in the office, furtively eating some sugar, she set upon him and boxed his ears. Yet a moment later she came back saying, "Why are you making a hog of yourself? Don't you have any sugar at home? Take this bag with you and get going!" Her manner had changed completely within a few minutes, but this was not being phony. What she sought was compliance, together with a clear display of her power. Her heartfelt concern and scolding attacks were not in the least inconsistent.

Wang Shouxin had not had an easy life. Her father had been a horse trader, with no property to fall back upon and no regular job. The powerful could cheat and oppress him; yet honest people would also shy away from him. Wang Shouxin grew up with a fear of the Japanese, the collaborationist police, and everyone who owned wealth or land. Yet using her womanhood, which included a certain measure of good looks but excluded a sense of shame, she developed the weapons she needed for self-protection and for attack. Her environment taught her not to be shy, and she learned how to develop contacts with people whose social status was much higher than hers. She was obliged to adjust to hardship and could endure even inhuman living conditions. She became familiar with the lives of people at the lowest stratum of society. This was all very useful to her in the 1970s, when her life changed drastically.

After 1970, Bin County suddenly began to build all sorts of factories; the use of coal increased dramatically, while coal production remained the same. This phenomenon set the stage for Wang Shouxin to display her talents.

First she had to go to the appropriate prefectural and provincial offices to fight for the necessary allocations of coal and transportation facilities. No matter how high the official, she had a way of putting him at ease. She could summon every charm that a woman of fifty could muster without being disgusting. "Ahem, I say, Secretary Wang (or Manager Gao, or Secretary-General Nie, or whatever), we common folk in Bin County are in quite a fix. We have to queue for coal and can only buy small baskets of it. If you don't increase our allotment, we might have to burn our own legs . . ."

She'd cajole you, pester you, flatter you no end. One minute she'd laugh, the next she'd cry—all entirely in good faith. Still no answer? Fine, she had yet another trick: she'd undo her pants and give you a look at the scar on her abdomen, making it clear that Old Lady Wang was braving illness to come fight for the people's coal. Now how about it? Hadn't you better figure out a way to get her to pull up her pants? Worried, angry, you'd want to get rid of her as quickly as possible. But then you would think again—she *had* come for the public good, after all. And you had to hand it to her: her local flavor, her common touch, her ingenuousness (pants half-down, etc.), and her intimate manner did have a certain charm for men her age.

"OK, I'll approve 2,000 tons for you." As long as coal was for sale, it was all the same whether it went to Bin County or to Hulan. Old Lady Wang would leave overjoyed.

A few days later, someone would show up at the same official's office carrying a few things: ten pounds of fish, twenty pounds of pork, several dozen eggs, and a few quarts of soybean oil. At first the official would have no idea where they came from. But as the saying goes, show me the official who flogs gift-givers. What's more, these were all things that were hard to come by at any price. "How much a pound? How much should I pay altogether?" The bearer would only laugh—"What's your hurry? We'll take care of it later"—and leave.

At first all these things had to be purchased, and at high prices. A pound of fish cost over a dollar. But Wang Shouxin had vision. Buy it! She even had her own underground cold-storage cellar specially built, so that she could store things and have them at her disposal. Eventually things came by means of barter: a commune or a production brigade that made bricks would be given coal and, in exchange, would give her hogs, each one of which had to be at least 220 pounds with thin skin and lots of meat. As the scope of Wang Shouxin's exchanges widened, and as her needs increased, she had to figure out a way of increasing her sources of goods while lowering their cost. So she set up fishing teams of four men to a net, then constructed a hog farm, and then a "nonstaple foodstuffs base" that occupied the land of an entire production team and allowed her to produce fruits and vegetables for her private use. But Old Lady Wang still wasn't satisfied; she finagled a bulldozer that spent days noisily digging a great hole that she converted to a fish-farming pond.

Wang Shouxin's requirements kept on increasing as the County Party Committee gave her responsibility for buying cement, fertilizer, and tractors. Her responsibilities required ever more contact with higher and higher officials. Other than giving gifts, what means had she to "ignite" these people's "revolutionary zeal"?

Wang Shouxin was a keen observer of the lives of leading cadres both inside and outside the county. She knew their thinking and their needs. "Aside from eating," she mused to herself, "what other problems most worry them? What are they most concerned about?" Then, slapping her thigh, this extremely clever woman cried out, "I've got it! Their sons and daughters! They're always thinking of how to keep them from being sent down to the countryside, how to bring them back to town as soon as possible, how to get them into college or get them a better job!" Since so many places were setting up "camps for educated youths" who had been sent down to the countryside, why couldn't her fuel company set one up in the name of the production brigade? It could be, in effect, a transfer station. With Wang Shouxin's extensive network of connections, it would be no problem at all to get dozens of sons and daughters into college, or into good jobs, or transferred back to the city.

The location she decided upon was the Pine River Brigade of the Raven River Commune. There she had ten or so tile-roofed houses put up, and the scions of leading cadres at the provincial, prefectural, and county levels came in droves. Some didn't bother to come but had their names put down anyway. In either case these children drew a salary of thirty or forty dollars a month. Commissar Yang's daughter, whose name had been entered in this way, never worked a stitch but did get admitted to the Party and was later "transferred" back to Harbin.

While some laughed, others wept.

For example, here is one of the many letters of accusation that were written over a number of years by the peasants of the Pine River Brigade:

> . . . Wang Shouxin and her parasitical ilk have used their influence for years to oppress us; they have forced us to sell, or simply give to them, the most productive land of four of our production teams; they have destroyed as much as 143 acres of our forests. Our production brigade's brick kilns use her coal, so she had us in a stranglehold if we didn't give her the land. She and the others cut down over ten thousand of the pine trees we had planted with ten years of arduous labor. The 25 acres of terraced fields we carved out of the hillsides have been turned into her melon patch. And still they have the arrogance to boast that if they order production teams to be ploughing their fields by 6 A.M., even our Party secretary won't dare to miss an hour! The production team had to neglect their own land because they didn't dare to ignore Wang Shouxin's. Her people also sank a well near the terraced fields, and then locked it up, refusing to let the local peasants have any water! Because they've taken our good land and stolen our labor, we've been driven to the point where we get only 40 cents a day in pay. They never pay the agricultural production tax, nor any tax whatever on all their income—everything we produce is used for giving gifts to rotten cadres and throwing parties for them. . . .

Yet Wang Shouxin's conscience was clear. All these activities of hers were "for the public good." Why else would every County Party secretary she worked with praise her so effusively? "Old Lady Wang is really great!" they would say. "She's come up with so much coal!" "Old Lady Wang really gets results! Of all the five counties bordering the river, Bin County has shipped the greatest amount of coal!"

But there was one question: her money. Where did it come from?

There were two kinds of coal. Coal produced by the state-run coal mines had a sale price fixed according to the cost of producing it, and was supplied "under the state plan." Coal supplied "outside the state plan" was small-pit coal, and transport and miscellaneous charges were added to its price. From 1972 onward, Wang Shouxin hit upon an extremely simple scheme for making money: take a portion of the state coal and charge small-pit coal prices for it. This would net from three to nearly ten dollars per ton. She made out two sets of invoices: one bearing the original prices and another with transport and miscellaneous charges added. The latter were not entered in the accounts, nor was the extra money ever paid to the state.

Wang Shouxin let only two people in on her great secret. One was her accomplice Ma Zhanqing, director of White Rock Enterprises, which was part of the fuel company. The other was an accountant named Sun Xiyin. Both of them had been brought into the Party by Wang Shouxin. Sun Xiyin came from a family of small businessmen, and the only human relationship he thought possible was essentially that between shopkeeper and shop clerk, or perhaps between a Japanese and a collaborator. It was natural that he now treated Wang Shouxin with the same obsequiousness and loyalty he once gave to his shopkeeper. He was ever grateful to Secretary Wang for bringing him into the Party. He knew her orders were that income from the surcharges on small-pit coal be set aside in a special account and not be paid over to the state; invoices for it were to be destroyed. His own job was fourfold: making up invoices, collecting payment, keeping the books, and distributing coal. Thus, carrying out the secretary's orders came quite naturally to him.

One day, when Wang Shouxin had finished her instructions to him and Sun Xiyin had turned to go, she told him to stop. "Wait a minute. I hear you're going to tie the knot again? Tsk! You're all of fifty years old! Why bother with something like that? Forget it!" This was an order, but Sun Xiyin felt it had been well meant; the secretary was *so* concerned about him. In point of fact it had been nineteen years since his wife had died, and only after careful consideration had he decided to seek another companion.

What really concerned Wang Shouxin was her secret. There was nothing to be gained in involving another pair of ears and another mouth. Who could tell what kind of person Sun Xiyin had hooked up with? What could she do if this woman turned out to be as loose tongued as herself?

Her Party

Even after justice finally caught up with her, Wang Shouxin was known to have boasted. "Go to Bin County yourselves," she said.

"Old Lady Wang was tops at looking after the welfare of the masses!" This was not untrue. At her behest, her staff's coal and food was always delivered right to their homes. And there was always something extra at festival time. At Mid-Autumn Festival everyone got two pounds of mooncakes, but these Wang Shouxin delivered personally so that everyone would believe that Secretary Wang was favoring only him. This made one especially grateful. On a trip to see a doctor in Canton, Wang Shouxin was careful to remember to buy everyone a synthetic-fiber sweater. And the fuel company had built more worker housing than any other enterprise in the Bin County seat.

But Secretary Wang had another method of dealing with people: oral abuse. She could chew someone out so utterly, "to the depths of his soul," that after a few sentences the person would be in tears. Take Zhou Lu, for example—assistant manager, second-in-command, a tall, strapping fellow. Wang Shouxin abused him as if he were her child. She swore at him "as if he were a clove of garlic," as they said in the local dialect, or "as if he were an eggplant." When the staff showed up for work, one look at Zhou Lu's face would let them know if Secretary Wang was in or not. If Zhou Lu was busily going about his business, then Wang Shouxin was not in. If he had a straight face and acted as if he were scared of his own shadow—then Secretary Wang was definitely in. "I have come to this pass," Zhou Lu thought to himself, "because of only one thing—fear. Dealing with her I'm like a piece of bean curd that has fallen into a pile of ashes; you can't brush the ashes off, you can't blow them off— nothing works. My only hope lies in her age. How much longer can that candle of hers burn? Once she's dead I'll be all right."

Despite her tremendous capacity to terrorize, Wang Shouxin still could not rest easy. She always worried about who might be out to get her, and she had an extraordinarily sensitive intelligence network. At one point Zhou Lu, no longer able to put up with Wang Shouxin's temper, decided to resign as assistant manager and go back to driving a car. The next day Wang Shouxin took him to task. "So you want out, do you? If you want out, I'll give you your walking papers right now. Out! Get out right this minute!"

Her intelligence network had, of course, required painstaking cultivation. By crowding some people and getting them transferred out, then wheedling others and getting them transferred in, finally the staff of the fuel company was almost all people in whom Wang Shouxin could have complete faith. She simultaneously set about building a Party organization of foolproof reliability.

When Wang Shouxin discovered someone of acceptable obsequiousness, she'd drag him in and say: "Blind enthusiasm isn't enough; you must coordinate with the organization."

When the Party met to discuss the first person she nominated, some members disagreed with her choice. This made Wang Shouxin blow her stack. "He withstood the test of the Great Cultural Revolution! He's stronger than any of you! Look at you Party members! A bunch of capitalist-roaders and monarchists! Not one of you is worth a damn! If this man isn't fit for the Party, none of you is!"

She got her way. The second person she advanced was Ma Zhanqing. His credentials: ". . . exerts himself to the fullest, shouts slogans all day long, is very good at dispensing coal, is not too self-seeking, watches over public property like a hawk. I think he's all right, fit to be a Party member." Again some people opposed him, and Wang Shouxin's jaw dropped in disbelief. "If everyone in the fuel company were like Ma Zhanqing," she said, "we'd all be a lot better off!" Having spoken, she picked up her tobacco basket and left. This signaled that Ma Zhanqing had been accepted and that the meeting was adjourned.

Wang Shouxin single-handedly recruited eleven Party members. The special qualifications of each one merit careful scrutiny.

A driver: obedient, simple, straightforward. When ferrying Wang Shouxin around to deliver gifts, he continued to be simple and straightforward. Clearly he had some reservations, but he never leaked a word. And never asked any questions. He just stuck to one principle: "Nobody can question Secretary Wang's activities. Do what you like, but that is that."

Another: hard working, honest, obedient, eager to get into the Party. When Wang Shouxin was building a house for her sister, he sawed a publicly owned pine gangplank into six pieces and procured a case of glass that had been cut to proper size. He delivered these by truck to the building site.

A carpenter: hard working, honest, obedient. He took care of all the work that Wang Shouxin needed done on her own house. He was also adept at delivering gifts.

With one exception, the eleven Party members were all "hard

working, honest, obedient." Obedient to whom? To Wang Shouxin, of course. According to the logic that says that closely following the secretary is closely following the Party, and that protecting the secretary is protecting the Party, how far wrong were they, actually?

In short, Wang Shouxin had a rear guard in the fuel company upon whom she could depend. And in the County Party Committee and the County Revolutionary Committee, she had thirty-some "rebel" cohorts working for her like bees. From the County Party Standing Committee, and from the Party secretary personally, she had nothing but praise and trust. What more could Wang Shouxin ask? She was entering the prime of her career.

Of course, when she remembered her illicit treasury with its more than forty thousand crisp, new ten-yuan [about $6.70] bills, she became slightly nervous. At these times a certain image would appear in her mind and give her strength. "Ha, come to think of it, what do we little guys matter? Aren't the top cadres in the province always sticking their hands into the till?" She was thinking of the assistant manager of the Provincial Fuel Company, Guo Yucai. She had been going to him since 1971 whenever she needed coal; in return he received quite a lot of chicken, fish, meat, and eggs. Finally she invited him to White Rock Harbor, where she held a banquet especially in his honor. Having drunk and eaten his fill, Guo Yucai lay down on the bed-platform. "Remember those two trucks I got you?" he said. "I'm out of pocket quite a bit on them!" Wang Shouxin caught his drift immediately, wrapped up two hundred dollars, and handed them over to him. A few days later he came back again. "The last time I was in Beijing on business I was short of cash." Another few hundred made their way to him. Over a four-year period Guo Yucai took over $1300 in bribes; in return he assigned Bin County six trucks, a refueling machine, and a large amount of coal.

This man was precisely the type for Wang Shouxin. What she feared most was that other Communist Party members would prove to be unlike her, to have no greed. The more important the cadre, and the more gifts and money he took, the more elated she was. By going through Guo Yucai, Wang Shouxin was able to throw a banquet for a deputy head of a department in the Ministry of Commerce. When she saw him off at Harbin, Wang Shouxin presented this man with a set of sofas, a bed-wardrobe combination and tea tables, as well as 100 cubic feet of lumber and several gunny sacks of soybeans. He accepted everything. Wang Shouxin was now more at ease than ever. "Even in Beijing cadres are like this," she observed to herself. "These articles weren't Old Lady Wang's private property—he must have known that!"

When the Gang of Four fell from power, Wang Shouxin and her "rebel" comrades-in-arms felt a momentary quiver of fear. But for Wang Shouxin, the long trip she took in 1978 was evidence enough that, even though nearly two years had elapsed since the smashing of the Gang of Four, Old Lady Wang's position was not only as impregnable as ever, but even continuing to rise.

This long trip in 1978 was a show of strength, a demonstration of her power. It had been arranged for her by Vice–Secretary-General Nie of the Heilongjiang Provincial Economic Committee and was intended as thanks to Wang Shouxin for her help in arranging for his three children to return from the countryside and take jobs in the city. He had bought airline tickets for her and sent his son to accompany her. When this embezzler extraordinaire took off from Harbin airport, three department heads of the provincial government showed up to see her off. When she arrived in Canton, three units were there to receive her. In Shanghai, someone was specially sent to take her to a first-class hotel.

Wang Shouxin had reached the pinnacle of wealth and fame. Her influence "at the top" was growing daily. The car of some provincial, prefectural, or county official was always in front of her house. Her status had skyrocketed because of the many things she had been able to procure for Bin County, and as her status rose, she became ever more fearless, arrogant, and oppressive. In tiny Bin County, whom should she fear?

"All-out Dictatorship"

At the beginning of 1975, while it was still winter, Wang Shouxin and some workers climbed the mountains of Gaoleng in search of timber. They headed into the hills with pork, hard liquor, cigarettes, and soap in their trucks. At each checkpoint Old Lady Wang would go in for a friendly exchange, while her henchmen outside began giving out all those things that were normally so hard to find. At some checkpoints Old Lady Wang would go in, put down her carry-all, and say with generosity and concern, "Didn't I hear that you were short of batteries here? Here, I've brought some flashlights to go along with them!"

In the hills she and her henchmen paid off the inspectors. Old Lady Wang feared no danger or difficulty; she led her troops without mishap up slippery heights of snow-covered piles of logs, picking out the best and calculating her total as she went. When her trucks returned full, all the checkpoints along the way let them pass without inspection once they knew it was Old Lady Wang. In this manner she got more than 1750 cubic feet of top-quality pine for just over $330.

This was a happy event, and Wang Shouxin planned to celebrate it. She could hardly have known that big trouble awaited her in Bin County. Inspector Yang Qing, of the County Disciplinary Inspection Committee, was looking for her. He revealed to her that a member of the County Standing Comittee had received an anonymous letter accusing Wang Shouxin of the crime of corruption. That night Wang Shouxin went to Yang Qing's house with two bottles of superior liquor and took possession of the accusing letter—so that, she said, she could check the handwriting.

The next day, as soon as Wang Shouxin arrived at work, she threw the letter down in front of Zhou Lu and began swearing at him. "Goddamn it to hell! I go to Gaoleng for twenty days to get timber and everything here turns upside-down! . . . What the hell have you been doing here? Didn't I tell you to keep your eye on these people?"

Inspector Yang Qing (who later became vice-chairman of the Disciplinary Inspection Committee) also came in, and together with Zhou Lu tried to identify the handwriting by comparing it with that used in other criticisms and complaints. Unfortunately nothing turned up, but Yang Qing picked up the offending letter and reassured Wang Shouxin. "Don't worry who wrote this," he said. "The letter's in my control now, and that will be that!" These words hinted darkly, and also promised, that he was putting on the market the power he had in his hands to shield a criminal. The buyer was there; it did not matter very much at what time the price would be paid.

"OK," said Wang Shouxin, affecting unconcern. "So this letter was aimed at me. A branch secretary has to expect such things. Let's just forget it. If it had been written about someone else, we'd have to be stricter!"

Yang Qing was as good as his word: the letter was never seen again. But Wang Shouxin was not going to leave things at that. She sent three telegrams in a row ordering that the driver Qu Zhaoguo be sent back from the Jixi Coal Mine, saying he was needed for military training. Qu Zhaoguo hurried back that very night. As he entered the room, before he could even take off his padded jacket, he was blasted by Wang Shouxin: "You wanted to grab power from me? You were going to plant a bomb under my ass that would blow me to kingdom come?"

Qu Zhaoguo was utterly floored. He had driven on Wang Shouxin's gift-giving missions a long time now; he even called himself "Old Lady Wang's aide-de-camp." Every parcel, big or small, was personally delivered by this "aide-de-camp." He made sure nobody got the wrong parcel, but never asked any irrelevant questions, either. He was only a silent observer. For example, he noticed that nearly all the houses to which he delivered gifts had telephones. This proved they were occupied by pretty high officials. Wang Shouxin was correct in suspecting that he had been able to guess her secrets. Once when they went to the Provincial Fuel Company seeking coal, he heard an accountant ask Wang Shouxin if she could possibly get him some ready cash, say $3,500 or so. He also heard Wang Shouxin's reply. "Is $3,500 enough? I'll give you $7,000!"

"You can disburse that much?" asked the accountant.

"I don't have to disburse it," replied Wang Shouxin. "There's that much at White Rock."

Qu Zhaoguo was surprised to hear this but immediately composed himself and pretended not to have heard it. This was the first time the secret of the illicit treasury at White Rock had leaked out. Four years later, when the Bin County Party Committee sent a work team to the fuel company to investigate, three months of hard work failed to disclose Wang Shouxin's fatal secret.

Once Wang Shouxin sent down an order that everyone in the fuel company participate in "study sessions." First they would study those two long articles by Zhang Chunqiao and Yao Wenyuan.[6] And this was indeed fitting, for Wang Shouxin was already quite "dictato-

---

6. Presumably "On All-out Dictatorship Over the Bourgeoisie," by Zhang Chunqiao, in *Red Flag*, no. 4, 1975, and "On the Social Basis of Lin Biao's Anti-Party Clique," by Yao Wenyuan in *Red Flag*, no. 3, 1975. *Red Flag* is the theoretical journal of the Central Committee of the Communist Party. Zhang and Yao were leading Party theorists, and two of the Gang of Four.

rial"—more than that, she wanted to be "all-out" dictatorial. Next they studied Xiaojinzhuang [a model commune], and everyone was asked to write criticisms of the bad people. Wang Shouxin took these to her office and checked them closely, one by one, trying to see whether any matched the handwriting of the accusatory letter.

Next everyone studied Xiaojinzhuang's "poetry contest." Wang Shouxin made the opening statement, which was also a kind of call to arms. "Our fuel company has turned up a Fu Zhigao!"[7] she said, stroking her raven-black hair. She liked to compare herself to Jiang Jie.[8] "What's so bad about our company? Even if something is wrong, can't we take care of it ourselves, without writing secret letters of accusation? . . . I'm a fifty-some-year-old woman, why should I bother to get up early, or burn the midnight oil? Everybody knows this old lady keeps on working, illness or no illness . . ." As she spoke she began loosening her belt, and some men who knew what was coming up next quickly lowered their heads. But she couldn't undo her belt that day, probably because she was so agitated. "Have I, Wang Shouxin, ever failed you?" she continued. She cried, swearing and cursing, "The person who wrote that letter will come to no good end! If he has two sons, may they both die! If he has two daughters, may they both die! Extinction to his family!"

The atmosphere at the "poetry contest" was extremely tense. On one side the drum began pounding fiercely, as if Zhang Fei[9] were about to jump out. As the drumbeats quickened, a handkerchief was passed around. Everyone passed it as quickly as possible, as if it could burn one's fingers; the rule was that whoever had it in his hand when the drum stopped had to compose a poem. Candy and apples were set out on the table, but no one was in the mood to eat anything.

The first set of poems attacked Lin Biao and Confucius. Then they became more and more outrageous, using language that would not pass a swineherd's lips. This poem was among the more civilized:

> His family are Japs, and Soviets, too,
> American bones, the flesh of a Jew,

---

7. A traitor in the widely read novel *Red Crag* (1961) by Luo Guangbin and Yang Yiren.

8. The martyred heroine of *Red Crag*.

9. Fearless military hero in the *Romance of the Three Kingdoms* and other stories, whose entrance in Peking operas is always announced by drumrolls.

And who may this be? I hear you ask,
His name is Wan, and he ain't worth a screw!

This poem amused Wang Shouxin, and elicited a giggle from her. It was only when she giggled that anyone else dared to.

The next poet clearly had foreknowledge of Wang Shouxin's intentions, since he caricatured Qu Zhaoguo:

Five-foot-six, tall for a runt, mouth as big as
   his mother's _____,
Hatchet-face, pointy chin, turtle's neck,
   legs long and thin,
Smiles as though he's hard at work, really only
   knows how to shirk.
Carries a notebook in his clothes, whatever happens,
   the notebook knows,
And he can use it, to wail and complain, every time
   there comes a campaign.
The Party branch he wants to unload,
   and make his way down the capitalist road!

Wang Shouxin laughed as she listened, then tossed the poet an apple and some candy to show her approval. As soon as the poem had been read, she assumed a serious expression.

"Qu Zhaoguo, stand up!" she bellowed. Qu Zhaoguo drew up his five feet six inches and stuck out that neck upon which so much obloquy had been laid. He moved to the center of the room.

Wang Shouxin still was not finished. "If a man has a good wife at home he won't do anything dumb. Lu Yaqin, you lousy little flirt, stand next to him!"

Lu Yaqin refused to stand up. "Call in the militia!" shouted Wang Shouxin. "The only reason we maintain an army is so we can use it when we need it!" But the militia wouldn't budge. "You're on her side?" Wang Shouxin turned around and suddenly became pleasant and agreeable.

"Zhaoguo, I say, if you wrote the letter, why don't you just admit it?"

"I didn't write it, so how can I admit it? And even if I had written it, it's no vicious attack, and not directed at Party Central. What is there to fear?"

The beating of the drum began again, and once again everybody began writing poems. Their hearts were beating like the drum, thump, thump, thump. These were people who heaved coal all day long—how could they be forced to write poems? Some of them racked their brains until the sweat poured out; for the rest of their lives they would tremble whenever they heard a poem read. But if you didn't write a poem, if you didn't vilify someone, you would become the focus of suspicion—and that was no laughing matter. Some people stole behind the backs of others to see what kind of poems they were writing. People with no education, who couldn't come up with anything, could only stand up and recite "prose"—usually a string of nasty obscenities.

Oh, motherland, are these the masters of the People's Republic? The proletariat whose dictatorship we have? Is this our working class?

Wang Shouxin—is she in the vanguard of the working class, of the Communist Party?

In what colors should we paint this chapter of our history?

Spinelessness: The Disease of the Times

The fuel company was only 220 yards away from the headquarters of the County Party Committee. If the committee could not hear the sounds of Wang Shouxin cursing and the workers weeping, could they really have missed that beating drum? Not seen the big-character posters, or any of the accusatory letters? What about the letters of complaint relayed down to them several times from the provincial and prefectural Party Committees? Had they never seen or heard any of these things?

To leaf through the minutes of the County Party Committee meetings from 1972 onward is an intensely depressing experience. All sorts of problems are discussed: military conscription, family planning, criminal sentences, sowing plans—but hardly any mention of the problems of the Party itself. The Communist Party regulated everything, but would not regulate the Communist Party.

Nineteen seventy-two certainly was an historic year in modern Chinese history. In Bin County, cadres' banqueting and drinking—and pilfering, grabbing, embezzling, and appropriating—all reached a new high that year. And it was in 1972 that Wang Shouxin launched her corruption on a grand scale. The County Party Committee was officially restored in this same year, and Liu Zhen came to Bin County as the first in the succession of First Party Secretaries after the Cultural Revolution.

Even before Liu Zhen moved in, Wang Shouxin dispatched people to put up wooden screens in his house and to deliver shiny black lump coal and, later, top-quality rice. Since they were neighbors they had some other contact as well, but there is no way to establish that Liu Zhen cooperated in, or tried to cover up, Wang Shouxin's criminal activities. When he left in 1976 for another post, he actually warned the woman who succeeded him as secretary that "you should watch out for this Wang Shouxin—she doesn't play straight."

This shows that Liu Zhen had sharp eyes; he could also figure things out. What he lacked was a certain amount of something else.

The problem was that he was as agreeable as could be. Whether lecturing at a meeting, greeting guests, or simply walking along the street, he always had a smile on his face. His gestures, voice, manner, and walk were all gentle and mellow, as if always and everywhere he sought to show others that "I have nothing against anyone; please don't get me wrong, I wouldn't offend or harm anyone." Even people who were dissatisfied and full of gripes would never lose their tempers at Secretary Liu, because of the deep sympathy that welled up behind his rimless eyeglasses. He would listen to your appeal with the utmost concern and attentiveness, as if ready to do anything in his power to satisfy whatever request you made. In reality, of course, he never got anything done.

Before long he got a nickname: "The Old Lady Official." And another: "Liu Ha-ha." He would always nod his head and say, "Ha-ha, fine, fine, fine." Once he returned home and his wife sadly told him that the chickens they had been raising had all died from a disease. "Ha-ha, fine, fine, fine," he replied.

Was he born with this kind of character? Probably not. If one attributes such things to nature, one has to account for a remarkable coincidence. Why is such nature so concentrated? Why, out of three current members in the County Party Secretariat, were all three notoriously "slippery" and "treacherous"?

When the Cultural Revolution began, Liu Zhen had been the County Party secretary of Shuangcheng County. His soul (not to mention his body) had been a little too deeply "touched"—to the point where he had been badly scarred by the experience. Before he

came to Bin County, he had been warned: "That place is very complicated; few have gone in there and come out unscathed"; "Bin
County—it's scarcely possible to investigate a single thing there." He
had long heard that violent struggle and false accusations had left
more people dead in Bin County than anywhere else in the prefec-
ture.

The previous County Party secretary, Zhang Xiangling, had given
Liu a detailed introduction to the "rebels" and had warned him point-
edly not to rely on rebel leaders such as Wen Feng.

Liu Zhen listened and nodded his head; but his own thoughts were
running in the opposite direction: "This guy has offended a good
many people. If I don't improve relations with the 'rebels', how can I
establish myself? Isn't this as clear as can be?"

Not long after that, Liu Zhen restored the respectability of the
belly-aching Wen Feng, who had been relegated to work in Binzhou
by Zhang Xiangling, by putting Wen Feng on the Standing Committee of the County Revolutionary Committee. The rest of Wen Feng's
clique were given new positions as well.

In 1972, not long after the County Party Committee had been restored, everyone on the Standing Committee pointed out that one
thing was perfectly clear: the greatest problems with current Party
leadership were an unwillingness to combat unwholesome tenden-
cies and a lack of fighting spirit. The secretary and Standing Committee even devised such resounding slogans as "Work hard, change
quickly; the first to change must be the county headquarters!" and
"Whether we can change or not depends crucially upon whether the
county headquarters can change!"

Three years later, the 1975 Standing Committee again came to investigate, and the problem was still the same: nobody dared to fight
back. And why was this? "Afraid of getting caught in a quagmire,
afraid of offending others, afraid of stirring up a hornet's nest . . ."

Another four years passed—1979—and Wang Shouxin had finally
been indicted. When the Standing Committee came yet again to investigate, there was still the problem of "being afraid to struggle."

Did this reluctance to speak up come from everyone's having been
bought out by criminals such as Wang Shouxin? Of the eleven members of the Standing Committee of the County Party Committee, nine
had accepted Wang Shouxin's gifts—this was a fact. Nonetheless,
there were some among the leading cadres who had never taken any

gifts. For example, the chairman of the County Disciplinary Inspection Committee was clean. Among the two or three hundred people to whom Wang Shouxin had given gifts, this woman was the only one who had resisted, the only one who had not been tainted. She was an upstanding comrade who had been working for the revolution since 1946, and she despised all the pulling and fawning around her. When she saw that people these days "couldn't tell right from wrong" or felt "doing one's job is a cinch, but building up good connections is hard," she was upset. "When will we ever be able to resolve this problem?" she worried. Yet even such a fine comrade as she still "failed to see" that people like herself would have to step forward if the problem was to be solved. She was humble, careful, diligent, conscientious, hard working and plain living—except for her unwillingness to struggle, she was the very image of a "good cadre."

Even though the Gang of Four had fallen, the County Party Committee was as weak and pusillanimous as ever in the face of the "rebels." In Bin County, the campaign to "expose, criticize, and investigate" was not carried out until 1978. This time around Wen Feng couldn't avoid self-criticism. But oh, what disappointments those mass criticism sessions were to the cadres and masses of Bin County! The language, tone, and content of the first self-criticisms were no different from regular reports. Secretary Guan was chairing the meeting, and everyone was waiting for him to give some indication of his attitude. But he wouldn't! With the second batch of self-criticisms it was no different: Secretary Guan still gave no indication of his attitude. This was highly unusual. People in Bin County had all become experts on political movements by then, and they felt that consistency with precedent should require the chairman to exert a little more pressure than this. But he still wouldn't! The third mass meeting was the most puzzling of all. At that time it had already been announced that Wen Feng had been relieved of his job and had handed over the reins; at the meeting, it ought to have been someone else's turn for self-criticism. Wen Feng was sitting at the back of the meeting hall that day. Everyone watched as Secretary Guan sent someone from the Organization Department back to the last row to ask Wen Feng up to the stage. Wen Feng was embarrassed and could not be persuaded to come forward. The next scene in this little drama was something nobody, including Wen Feng, was prepared for: Secretary Guan himself came down from the stage and walked the length of the hall, like an emperor leading his troops, right to the back row to give Wen Feng a personal invitation. He insisted on nothing less than having this worthless clod go up and take his place with the assembled leaders. This set the whole place buzzing. No one could understand it: "Isn't this thwarting the will of the people?" "Isn't this giving support to Wen Feng's clique?" Quite a few people felt concern for Secretary Guan: "Hey, Old Guan," they thought to themselves, "What are you doing? Aren't you afraid of losing face before the entire county?" Everyone felt disappointed and hurt. Old Guan had been around in Bin County since land reform [1945] and was well known for his bravery and staunch resolve in struggles with the enemy. He had been nicknamed "Guan the Ruthless," and this was an honorable epithet. Everyone thought of him as one of the more trustworthy members of the County Party Committee. When the Wang Shouxin affair came to light, everyone said privately that "no matter how many at county headquarters are implicated, Guan the Ruthless won't be one of them." But now, how could he have disappointed everyone by doing what he had just done?

The Standing Committee and the secretaries were full of explanations for their easy treatment of the "rebels," including Wang Shouxin. One of them said in a self-criticism that the "Unified Program to Defend Mao Zedong Thought" had first liberated him and then "joined" with him. He had felt great gratitude for this. Another secretary had offered precisely the opposite explanation. The "rebels" had persecuted him, and he was afraid people would think he was seeking revenge. This had been why he refused to oppose the "rebels." In reality, the basic reason was clearly that the rebels had all along been a political force that no one could take lightly.

In sum, everybody feared offending this group or that group, but was quite happy offending the "masters" of our People's Republic— the people!

Among the various County Party secretaries, one person deserves separate mention because of the special circumstances of his case.

Wei Gao was one of three members of the County Party Committee between 1972 and 1976 whose credentials stood out from all the others. These three were all known for being "slippery" and for their great fondness for wine. At a meeting of the County Party Committee's Standing Committee in 1972, Wei Gao was evaluated as "evasive in all matters, always among the last to make his position known."

He was always trying to please every faction; matters of principle could go either way with him; he would always prefer to take one step backward in order to preserve the peace, rather than considering the bad effects such an action would have on important projects. Yet he did have strong points: he could view problems from many angles and was very good at consulting others.

At that time, he was the secretary in charge of the county's finance and trade; as Wang Shouxin's superior, he knew her like the back of his hand. After close observation and considerable thought, he decided to join his family and Wang Shouxin's through matrimony.

Wei Gao and his wife went together to see a matchmaker. His wife spoke first, asking Old Lady You to introduce their daughter Xiaoxia to Wang Shouxin's youngest son, Liu Zhizhong. But Old Lady You had her reservations. "Secretary Wei," she said, "your official star is shining its brightest; why do you think you need an old lady like me to make a match for you? Haven't you got offers all over the place?"

The couple insisted that they wanted the matchmaker to go ahead, so she said, "Do you know the background of their family very well? . . . Wang Shouxin and I are both originally from Manjing; when she was young she wasn't a very proper . . ."

"That was all a long time ago," Wei Gao interrupted. "Now that she's older, she doesn't act that way anymore."

So Old Lady You finally gave in. "OK, if you really want to hook up with a deadbeat family, I'll go do it for you."

Wei Gao and his wife took the initiative of going with their daughter to call on the Wang family elders. Later the couple went to the photography studio to visit their future son-in-law, who was a vice-chairman of the studio's Revolutionary Committee. Wang Shouxin was ambivalent about the match, thinking that the girl was not pretty enough.

The wedding was held quietly; even some of the County Party secretaries, when they heard of the nuptials after the fact, were puzzled. Why did Wei Gao insist on marrying into Wang Shouxin's family? This was not a good match.

The vice-chairman of the County Planning Committee, Yi Yong-quan, once accompanied Wei Gao to a meeting in Harbin and took this opportunity to speak to Wei Gao about Wang Shouxin. "As a secretary you're the ranking official in the county, but you will also be expected to give help to your daughter's mother-in-law . . . She has quite a reputation, you know, for throwing parties and giving gifts, squandering money and wasting resources. She's fouled the atmosphere with her corruption . . ." Li Yongquan cited many examples, observing Wei Gao's reaction as he spoke. Wei Gao gave no hint of his emotions, but Li could see clearly that he already knew all about these things and that he had basically determined not to concern himself with them. He finally replied by saying, "All this is hard to believe."

Li Yongquan immediately regretted his candor. He now realized that this fellow's reputation was well deserved, that he really was a sly old fox. Just look at that reply of his: he didn't deny that there was a problem with Wang Shouxin, but neither did he affirm that this was the case.

Perhaps it was due to his slyness that for a period of seven long years people were always wont to believe that the marriage match had been arranged by Wang Shouxin for the purpose of securing a dependable fallback. Not until half a year after Wang Shouxin's case had been cracked did the real truth come to light: Wei Gao had set his sights on Wang Shouxin's money.

The Reasons? Right under Our Noses!

The exposure of Wang Shouxin's case shocked the entire country. How could such a crude, shallow housewife muster such boldness and such ability? How could such brazen criminal activity go uninvestigated for so many years? From their common sense and intuition people naturally focused their attention on the Bin County Party leadership: they were at the root of this, they were her accomplices, it was they who had protected Wang Shouxin!

This is, to be sure, the impression one gets when one views Wang Shouxin's case in isolation from the economic, political, and social life of Bin County. But if one looks at the whole living organism, with Wang Shouxin and her criminal activity organically linked by a maze of arterial connections to the rest of life, then the situation appears to be very different.

Viewing the situation organically, one discovers the following: were it not for the illicit treasury in which she held cash amounting to over a third of a million dollars, Wang Shouxin and her activities would never have aroused the attention, or caused the shock, that they did when the full extent of her corruption was exposed.

Instead, what appears, continuing to view things in this way, is only this: a plainly dressed old lady, straight talking and industrious, rushing all day around Bin County and even outside of it, trying to gather coal, trucks, fertilizer, and cement for the benefit of the whole county.

Her party-throwing and gift-giving were carried out on a grand scale. But what officials were *not* throwing parties and giving gifts? The maxim "Without proper greasing, nothing works" is as true today as ever. Trucks carting nonstaple foodstuffs sped from the fuel company along the highway from Bin County to Harbin. But they were not alone. Trucks from the Bin County distillery, full of "Binzhou Liquor," traveled the same road, as did trucks from the fruit company carrying apples for the higher-ups. Even within Bin County itself, all the economic units would "pay tribute" to each other. Wang Shouxin's nonstaple foodstuffs base, sanitorium, and lavish banquets at White Rock were famous. But practically every section in Bin County had its own small dining hall, guest house, and storehouse. Parties with huge meals and lots of drinking went on everywhere! Wang Shouxin may indeed have been the Coal Queen of Bin County, but she most certainly was not alone. Bin County also had an Electricity King, the head of the electricity board, who was also called "the millionaire." This man's gift-giving and lavish parties cost in the neighborhood of $10,000 each year. Just as did Wang Shouxin's fuel company, the electricity board had to pay tribute to higher-ups.

Back in 1964, County Party Secretary Tian Fengshan had determined to put a stop to this wining and dining, but the result was only a brief interlude between periods of business as usual. After 1970, Zhang Xiangling also took up the cause; yet, ironically, wining and dining actually increased during his term in office. The integrity of these two secretaries and their revolutionary will to struggle were beyond any question. But neither one of them could achieve his end. The County Party Committee had gone so far as to pass a specific regulation, which was in force from 1972, stipulating that for official guests, no meal should have more than four courses and no liquor could be served. This rule was never actually put into effect. Every year the official county guest houses misappropriated $1300 of their budgets for this sort of entertainment. Each of these guest houses, which were run by the various departments of the County Revolutionary Committee, used its income to support the lavish gluttony of cadres. And besides serving their own gluttony, the cadres also dipped their hands into the till. It was, moreover, not only the cadres themselves who gourmandized and stole; their families did the same. At one time the County Party Committee ordered that such guest houses be closed, but to no avail.

Obvious as it was that Wang Shouxin had embezzled public funds to build her houses, the bricks and tiles themselves bore no record of her corruption. And there were many other houses built through embezzlement of various sorts. Aren't those who live in these houses resting easily in their good fortune even today, with no fear that they might ever be prosecuted for their misdeeds? A prime example is the new house of Yang So-and-so, Party secretary and manager of the biggest factory in Bin County, the towel factory.

Yang's house had originally been a structure attached to the factory. Because it had been built to purify water, the structure was fairly crude and had a tank on top of it. But Yang, on his own authority, decided that the structure needed major improvements, which would require tearing down the water tank. He then converted this industrial building into his own private residence. The four-room house required twenty-one tons of cement, not to mention other building materials.

This Yang was unlike Wang Shouxin only in that he used the state's materials and labor instead of its currency. In the final analysis there is no difference between the two.

So we can see that Wang Shouxin's criminal activities were, in the first place, covered up by the general decline in social morality, by the gradual legalization of criminal activity, and by the people's gradual acclimatization to the moral decay around them. Even the distinction between legal and illegal had become quite blurred. Where was the borderline between legitimate gift-giving and the offering and acceptance of bribes? Was using public funds for wining and dining or for converting public property to one's own use (as in requiring a "test use," or a "test wearing," or a "taste test") any different from corruption and robbery? The former was within the law, even considered morally sound, but in essence was no different from bribery and corruption. And misappropriation of public property was far more widespread than bribery or corrupt conduct.

There is yet more to discover about the residence of this Yang: there was no way his four-room house could have used twenty-one tons of cement, even though it turned out upon further investigation that, in violation of the regulations then in effect, he had had the walls of his house covered with a thick layer of cement so that the white plaster dust would not rub off. What really happened was that the head of the industrial section, a certain Du, was building his own residence at the same time. A large amount of building materials and half-finished articles "got lost" at the site of Yang's building. The two residences were completed one after the other, and the personal relationship between Yang and Du became even more intimate.

This "relationship" needs further consideration and analysis. Section Chief Du had protected, and would continue to protect, Factory Head Yang; Factory Head Yang, for his part, had supported and would continue to support Section Chief Du. But it was more than a two-party relationship; both Yang and Du had cliques surrounding them. And Yang had an addiction: beginning with his work at the county labor union in the 1960s, through several job changes leading to his present one at the towel factory, in each place he engaged in extramarital sex. Yet he could always come away untainted—like a duck waddling out of the water with its feathers dry. How did he do it? Section Chief Du had the same addiction, but he was quite different in the way he went about satisfying it. He cared not whom he harmed if a person blocked his way or knew too much. At least two framings were his doing, and he even insured that it would be a long time before the innocent victims were exonerated. And how did *he* do it? The same way: people, connections.

Many of the middle- to upper-level cadres in Bin County came from rural villages after the land reform of 1945. By the late 1960s and early 1970s, their sons and daughters were of marriageable age. The county seat of Bin County had only slightly more than 30,000 residents, and the number from the social levels appropriate for marriage to cadres was even smaller. Thus in-law relationships, and in-laws-of-in-laws relationships, came to overlie relationships that were already doing quite well—such as those of family, clan, friends, former classmates, former colleagues, former bosses or subordinates, or "I'll-scratch-your-back-if-you'll-scratch-mine" partnerships—and invested all of them with new importance. In terms of extent alone, these in-law relationships had become twice as important as they ever were in feudal society.

A change of equal importance (not to say of even greater importance) was the new layer of political relationships imposed upon personal relations by the Great Cultural Revolution. Those who belonged to the same "faction" shared each other's tribulations, shielded each other, and in a few short years became like brothers to people who had started out as total strangers! When they met and greeted each other as "elder brother" or "younger brother," they really meant it; the relationships between Communist Party members and between revolutionary comrades paled by comparison.

"In Bin County, it's hard to figure out how people are related. It's as though they carry special switches with them, and if you get involved with one person, you're suddenly involved with a whole network." When people who had lived in Bin County for a certain time explained their county to outsiders, they would begin with this phenomenon.

In 1972, a member of the County Party Standing Committee who had come from elsewhere expressed his feelings thus: "We must practice Marxism-Leninism, but there are many pitfalls in doing so. How could personal relationships get so complicated! If you try to go by the book, all sorts of difficulties crop up. You're sure to get dragged in by one thing or another. No matter what you do, somebody will take offense, some problem will arise. There are so many riddles, so much to untangle."

When the County Party Standing Committee met, even if it met in some place as confidential as the War Room of the Military Department, any discussion of personnel questions would inevitably reach the ears of the persons involved. This presented major difficulties for the cadres involved in allocating and transferring personnel. If they were still deliberating on someone's placement, or had just decided it, and that person got wind of the decision, he could come to appeal, or to raise protests, or to seek support from friends. Things often ended in a stalemate.

When someone got into trouble, ten people would intercede for him. When a complaint came in, all concerned would seek the good offices of others. If someone were to come and say to you that So-and-so and So-and-so have already agreed to help, and all we need now is you—what would you do? Would you adhere to the rules? And risk offending everyone in sight? Wouldn't it be better to cast a blind eye, give him a little wave of the hand and let him have his way this once? Unless one's Party discipline were exceptional, who would be such an ogre as to refuse?

Some people sum it up by saying that everything in China has been messed up by people who are afraid of offending others.

For the same reason a very strange phenomenon would occur time and again. Something of considerable gravity would take place and raise a tumult in the town. Everyone would insist that something be done about it. Yet as soon as somebody was sent to investigate, the whole affair would evaporate. In 1972, people from Manjing reported that an official named Chen, who was in charge of the supply and marketing cooperative, was constantly being wined and dined and having illicit relations with women. The problem was "serious." Since this cooperative was serving as an official model for the whole province at that time, something definitely had to be done. The local Standing Committee consulted with their secretary and decided to send someone to investigate. After a time the report arrived: "no great cause for alarm." Seven years later it came out that this fellow named Chen was guilty of embezzlement and had indeed been engaging in illicit sex for quite some time.

During this period, political movements were launched year after year in Bin County, but one thing was mystifying. As all these movements, or class struggles, as they were also called, became fiercer and fiercer, the evildoers felt more and more at ease. It was the good people who kept being victimized. Some were unjustly framed; others were subjected to attack and revenge for their exposure of evildoers.

Complex personal relationships, built of layer upon layer of interlocking connections, formed a dense net. Any Marxist-Leninist principle, any Party plan or policy that came into contact with this net would be struck dead, as if electrocuted. When an enterprise got entangled in the net, its socialist design would come undone; when a legal case fell into the net, the dictatorship of the proletariat would get twisted out of shape. Right and wrong became thoroughly confused, reward and punishment turned upside-down. Truth yielded to falsity; the good-hearted were ruled by the vicious.

"Why do good people look bad and bad people look good?" At one time this topic was actually discussed at a meeting of the Party Standing Committee. In reality, of course, much more was at stake than merely looking good or bad. What the masses said was, "In Bin County, the good are cowed while the evil are proud."

Just look at the great pride of that repeat offender Zhao Chun, who always managed to evade the law and go scot-free. From 1969 on, when this man used his relationship with the "rebels" to worm his way into the Party, he began brazenly stealing timber and other state-owned materials, committing crimes time after time. Each of these cases could have been investigated, but not once was he ever punished in any way. The County Party Committee had ruled that no one who owed money to the state could build a private house. He, though, not only owed the state money and lived in state-owned housing; he also was able to use state-owned building materials to build himself a second house. He stole building stones allocated for defense. When a tractor overturned, he siphoned off the compensation money for the dead driver's family, plus the money for repairing the tractor—over five thousand dollars—from the public treasury. He also sold the scaffolding that had been used in constructing this house and pocketed all the proceeds.

To this day Zhao Chun drives his car with reckless abandon. Sometimes he has intentionally aimed it toward Han Cheng, an official in the towel factory's security department, and has slammed on the brakes right in front of him. Zhao Chun's aim has been to threaten and torment this person who was in charge of prosecuting his crimes. "Just watch it, wise guy—remember I can kill you anytime I want!" This has been the unspoken message. The insults and vituperative obscenities he has hurled at Han Cheng have become so common that they are taken as a matter of course. And what about Han Cheng? Not only can he get no support, but he has been relieved of his job as a security official. When this happened he brought all the incriminating material from the many cases involving Zhao Chun to the authorities. He pleaded and appealed in every direction, but no one would touch the case.

Could anything be more blatant, more maddeningly perverse than this? But Han Cheng's was not the only case in Bin County of a security official being bullied by villains.

Why was it that even now, under the leadership of the Communist Party in socialist Bin County, and three whole years after the fall of the Gang of Four, this half-human half-monstrous behavior could continue unabated?

The riddle is easy to solve: Zhao Chun had "connections." Besides his "rebel" cohorts, he had a valuable uncle—Vice-Director Lu of the County Party Committee's Organization Department. Vice-Director Lu and Section Chief Du belonged to the same clique. As we have already seen, Section Chief Du and Manager Yang of the towel factory were also connected. And Manager Yang was the one who relieved Han Cheng of his job. Zhao Chun's several crimes had taken place in the towel factory; the tractor he destroyed and the compensation money he misappropriated were also written off by Manager Yang.

This lovely curtain of fraternal loyalty, sincere gratitude, mutual concern, profound friendship, etc., etc. concealed relationships of out-and-out power brokerage. One side would invest a peach (either a material benefit or the means to obtain one, derived, in either case, from the power in that side's own hands), and the other side would answer with a plum (also a material benefit either directly or indirectly returned).

This is another of the social conditions that created and helped cover up Wang Shouxin, and that continue even now to create and cover up criminal elements.

Little Guys Do Some Big Things

There were two minor figures in Bin County who dared to show their contempt for this all-encompassing, all-powerful net, and even dared to challenge it.

One was Liu Changchun, with whom we are already acquainted. Wang Shouxin looked down on him and often sneered at him behind his back, her mouth twisted in contempt. "Look at that miserable little twit!" she would say, and then spit. But she failed to realize how tough Liu Changchun's tiny, thin body could be. He could not be crushed by the awesome pressure brought to bear on him by the "rebels" and the army, nor was his fighting spirit worn down by long years of hard living and suffering. Liu Changchun's contribution to the final victory over Wang Shouxin cannot be underestimated.

First he was jailed as "anti-Army" and an "active counterrevolutionary"; later the charge was commuted to "bad element," and he was moved to a cell under the "civil administration" of his original unit. When he got out he had to do more than ten hours of hard labor per day, and was given only $14 a month for living expenses. His wife stayed at home, bedridden with acute heart disease. (The hospital denied her both medicine and doctors' services, a policy that had been ordered by Wang Shouxin's son Liu Zhizhong, who was vice-director of the Xinli Commune.) Finally, Liu Changchun was ordered to report to the countryside along with the cadres who faced elimination as "extra personnel." Liu Changchun was now up to his neck in debt and could borrow no more, so he had no alternative but to sell off his only remaining property—a two-and-a-half-room house. He got only $265 for it. After he was sent to the countryside his wife's illness worsened, and not long thereafter she died. He labored in a rural village for four and a half years, and of the more than one thousand persons sent there with him, Liu Changchun was the very last to get permission to return to Bin County.

By then Wang Shouxin had become a major figure in Bin County. Her home's furnishings and her standard of living were as good as those of a provincial Party secretary. She was constantly besieged by people bringing her gifts and asking her to do things. Liu Changchun had been left alone in the world—his wife dead and gone, his property wiped out, not a penny to his name.

Liu Changchun's life had come to this pass because of his stubbornness. He had already become unpopular during the fifteen or so years before the Cultural Revolution. He had always liked to speak up—about anybody.

When he returned from the countryside he was amazed at all the new houses Wang Shouxin had built. "Where'd she get this much money?" He began to investigate. He sought out Qu Zhaoguo, who liked to gossip; Qu revealed that Wang Shouxin had once lent $6,500 in cash to the provincial fuel company. When Qu was about to leave he scrutinized Liu Changchun carefully. Perceiving Liu's intentions, this smoothie Qu quickly calculated the balance of power involved.

"You think you can really get her?" he asked.

"That depends on whether she's done wrong!" Liu Changchun had not changed from earlier years. To see his spirit of determination and self-confidence you would have thought he was a prefectural Party secretary.

By this time Liu Changchun already suspected Wang Shouxin of corruption; his problem was to get reliable evidence. He had experience as a planner and statistician and knew that she could not have embezzled so much money merely through fraudulent "supplementary wages." He went looking for Old Battle-ax, the one who kept the fuel company's accounts.

"When you marked up the cost of nonstate coal," asked Liu, "how did you indicate it on the books? Was it obvious how much small-pit coal was sold on a given day?"

"No, it wasn't," replied Old Battle-ax. "Generally, they reported only the price of $16.50 per ton. There was no mention of the additional $10.10." Later he said, "In the accounting report that they made every ten days or so, they wrote at the bottom of each column: received, such-and-such an amount for transport charges of small-pit coal."

How were the invoices for coal made out? A person who had been employed at White Rock explained this to Liu Changchun. Two kinds of receipts were made out when coal was sold—one for the price of the coal and another for transport and miscellaneous charges. The latter receipts were never turned in; no one knew where they went.

"What, was it all embezzled?" Liu Changchun was beside himself.

"Who knows? They never let us find out . . ."

"That clinches it!" Liu Changchun did some mental arithmetic: 90,000 tons of coal a year, perhaps 10,000 tons of it sold as small-pit coal. That would generate an extra $100,000 per year—in five years that would be half a million dollars! But how to check this? Easy! Cast the net wide—ask each unit in the entire county to examine its receipts for coal purchases.

Liu Changchun's discovery encouraged him immensely. He pressed his investigations across the whole of Wang Shouxin's empire. How many potatoes and soybeans did she get from those hundred or more acres of land? How many fish did she get in one year from a labor force of four men? How much money could she embezzle from the supplementary wages of her temporary and seasonal labor?

At this point Yang Qing, vice-chairman of the Bin County Disciplinary Inspection Committee, betrayed Liu's activities to Wang Shouxin. As a non-Party member of the masses, Liu had been pursuing his work purely out of a sense of duty. He had given no thought to any personal gain from his endeavor and as later events made clear, he not only gained nothing but suffered a good deal because of it.

Liu Changchun was not alone. A second "little guy" to stir up the hornets' nest around Wang Shouxin was named Shi Huailiang, a worker in the pharmaceutical company.

Back in 1972 he had put up a wall poster entitled "Wang Shouxin Is the Key to Solving the Problems of Bin County." Where Shi Huailiang differed from Liu Changchun was in the somewhat broader scope of the questions he worried about and analyzed. He would occasionally come out with something quite surprising, but without much fuss beforehand. In 1972, for example, a brainstorm inspired him to mail seven dollars to Chairman Mao. "Enclosed are my Party dues," he wrote on the remittance form. "Please accept them, kind sir. Shi Huailiang."

This was indeed a strange act, and afterwards it brought him to the brink of disaster, because the remittance form was later sent back by some office. The leaders and Party members of the pharmaceutical company took Shi Huailiang to task. "Everybody knows you're no Party member, what do you mean trying to pay Party dues?" "What's the idea of sending Party dues to Chairman Mao?" The questioners supplied their own answers: one, "You're just itching to join the Party, and have itched yourself into a hopeless frenzy!"; two, "You are mentally ill."

How can "itching to join the Party" count as a crime? Only, obviously, if the applicant is joining for private gain rather than for the public good. But what possible basis could they have for assuming that Shi Huailiang wished to join for promotions and lucre rather than to devote himself to the cause of communism? They were seeing their own faults in someone else. But perhaps not. Perhaps their speculations accurately reflected a certain feature of objective reality: that joining the Party really could become, and in fact already had become, a well-known means to realize personal gain.

But wasn't this precisely what was worrying Shi Huailiang, precisely what made him send his Party dues directly to Chairman Mao? He had been applying for years to join the Party. But in the meantime there were certain things he couldn't understand. A person in the Xindian granary had been expelled from the Party only three months after joining, charged with illegally purchasing more than ten tons of state grain. A person in the County Grain Section had been expelled from the Party four months after joining, charged as a neo-bourgeois element. Another person had been detained for interrogation in solitary confinement three days after joining the Party. When the truth came out, it became clear that all these people had committed crimes before entering the Party. Then how was it that this sort of person could get into the Party? Once, during an official trip to Harbin and elsewhere, Shi Huailiang learned that quite a few who joined the Party did not go through proper channels but entered as "specially approved" members, all via "connections." "If this goes on for long," he mused to himself, "won't all these people inevitably change the nature of the Party? This is serious!" But how could he get this message to Chairman Mao? If he wrote a letter, Chairman Mao probably wouldn't receive it. Besides, think of the trouble if the letter fell into the wrong hands! He thought long and hard and finally came up with the idea of mailing his "Party dues" to Chairman Mao as a hint. Chairman Mao would surely wonder why this fellow hadn't paid his dues to the County Party Committee. "If he mailed them to me, there certainly must be some problem with the local Party." If Chairman Mao were to realize this and send down his instructions, Shi Huailiang could then let fly all his charges without fear of reprisals. He could send the authorities a report that would tell everything about the whole Bin County Party organization.

He had dreamed a lovely dream. But nothing came of it, and all he actually got for his efforts was a flurry of denunciations. The problems never reached the ears of the higher-ups. Yet this only reinforced Shi Huailiang's belief that the Party structure had suffered a breakdown that had to be corrected. His concern for things outside his purview was one of the symptoms of his "mental illness."

Shi Huailiang was different from Liu Changchun. Shi was much steadier, simpler, and more good-natured. He typically wore a silly grin on his face and did not look at all like the combative or cantankerous sort. His "mental illness" showed in his extraordinary sensitivity to the suffering of the masses. He seemed to reserve an extra nerve in constant readiness to pick up signals from strangers in need. He was a man of few words, unflappable and unhurried. The energy that others spent on talking he would devote to thought. Why was it, he wondered, that in 1976, when Bin County had had only one drought, a drought that hadn't even caused lower productivity (then still over 1130 lb./acre) they were already suffering from lack of food, clothing, and fuel? Why did there have to be national emergency allocations of money, food, and coal? Why was there a big drive in the county seat for contributions of winter clothing? Why, even with these measures, did so many peasant families have to burn the thatch from their roofs and the frames of their bed-platforms to get heat? How could it be that, after so many years of socialism, both collectives and individuals were as poor as this? . . . Every evening he spent a bit of time studying the works of Marx, Lenin, and Chairman Mao. Since his income was so low, he was able to buy only the thinner volumes. Yet he was already well versed in the *Anti-Dühring*.[10] Despite his poor education, he liked to write occasional reports on investigations of social phenomena, or the like, as if he were a researcher from the Bin County branch of the Chinese Academy of Social Sciences. This was no joke. There were plenty of people in Bin County more learned and literate than he, and plenty who were better writers, but Shi Huailiang was the only person anyone had ever known who considered unpaid social research to be his personal responsibility.

This being the case, it was quite natural that his attention should come to focus on the internal workings of the pharmaceutical company. As soon as it did, his life opened a new chapter whose title might have been "The Tragedy of Independent Thought: the Price of Concern for Country and People is Sacrifice of Oneself." Or: "A Good Person Almost Always Comes to Grief."

The first thing he observed at the pharmaceutical company was one aspect of the problem of "connections" that we have already discussed. From the time Secretary Pan arrived there, he began building his own little circles and cliques within the leadership. He drove out the old leadership one by one. Four of the five people in the new leadership weren't even members of the labor union! Then, after he had been secretary for two years, Secretary Pan suddenly struck it rich. When he arrived he had owed the public treasury more than $850, and two years later he had returned it all. Not only that, his son had bought a moped and a hunting rifle, and his family had turned up with expensive radios, clocks, watches, and so forth. Yet his salary was only $36.30 a month. Shi Huailiang continued to observe the personal relationships within the company, then gathered all his findings and wrote a wall poster:

> . . . how strange it is that a certain leader in our company, though he lives in a socialist society in the eighth decade of the twentieth century, dreams the dreams of an eighteenth-century feudal monarch. His doc-

---

10. *Anti-Dühring* is the brief title for Friedrich Engels' *Herr Eugen Dühring's Revolution in Science* (1878), an important work in clarifying basic theories of Marx.

trine is "I am king," and whoever disobeys him is in for trouble. The workers in the pharmaceutical company have none of the rights of citizens. They have become slaves. The leaders are doing whatever they please to the workers, and are subverting the nature of a collectively owned company . . .

When Shi Huailiang was preparing another wall poster, this one about Wang Shouxin, some people tried to dissuade him by saying, "Forget it—you can't do anything about them." But he only laughed and replied, "So what if I can't? History will record that there was somebody who opposed Wang Shouxin. That, too, has its uses."

On September 15, 1978, he wrote yet another wall poster that he took personally to glue up inside the County Party building. It was a very unusual poster, entitled "A Satellite for Social Science." It began thus:

> In the eighth decade of the twentieth century, several leaders of the Bin County Party Committee successfully launched a satellite for the "social bourgeoisie,"[11] thereby benefiting China's social sciences. The satellite not only provided valuable material for the scientific research of the Chinese Academy of Social Sciences; every socialist country in the world could, in my view, learn from its data. Wang Shouxin was in possession of neither factories nor land nor shops—no private means of production. Nonetheless, she was able to accumulate as much as $276,500 in cash and 900 kinds of material supplies. This qualifies hers as a rich and powerful family. In my view the phenomenon of Wang Shouxin has to have its scientific explanation; otherwise it would not have come into existence. I conclude that a dissection and analysis of it will promote the development of human society and of social science. Accordingly I call upon all the successive leaders of the County Party Committee who have been implicated with Wang Shouxin (but I exclude Zhang Xiangling), plus the various section and bureau chiefs who are also involved: Do not be afraid, and lift your sights above the question of your own culpability. Consider the fate of Party and country. Report the whole story, in simple, unadorned truth, to the provincial and central authorities. Summarize the lessons to be learned . . .

This was a most beneficial and necessary wall poster.

---

11. "Social bourgeoisie" refers to people who act like the bourgeoisie within the socialist system. It is not a standard term, but is parallel to "social imperialists," which in the 1970s was a standard term for the Soviet leadership, who were charged with acting like imperialists within a socialist system.

Joy Lined with Worry

In 1978, Bin County began its "Double Strike" campaign.[12] On August 1, the first wall poster attacking Wang Shouxin for corruption appeared. This was the work of Liu Changchun again!

On August 5, a work team from the County Party Committee stationed itself at the fuel company. This time it seemed the County Party Committee really meant business. Yet while the battle was ending in victory, it was also revealing some problems.

When a Communist Party county committee dispatches a work team to look into the problems of an enterprise over which it is charged with leadership, how can this work team receive no support from the local Party organization? From start to finish, not a single Communist Party member came forward to expose Wang Shouxin to the work team.

The work team leader, Gu Zhuo, was a clear-headed and capable comrade. He and many of his team worked so hard that they gave up sleep and lost weight. Yet even after three months they could uncover no material that conclusively proved Wang Shouxin's corruption.

Comrade Gu Zhuo acknowledged that the only important information supplied to his work team during the investigation came from the same Liu Changchun. Liu was also the only one to take the initiative in providing information. Flush with excitement, he had told Gu Zhuo that "Wang Shouxin's den is at White Rock." (Later, hundreds of thousands of dollars did indeed turn up in her illicit treasury at the White Rock Business Department.) "She sells state-enterprise coal as small-pit coal and marks up the price. You can have my head if she isn't guilty of corruption! I think she may be the biggest embezzler in the entire country."

"Enough, enough!" Gu Zhuo had been thinking to himself, quite unconvinced. But the facts eventually showed that every word Liu Changchun had said was true.

Gu Zhuo had bridled at what Liu Changchun said next. "I've told all this to Secretary Guan and to the provincial and prefectural leaders. If you don't clear things up here you'll have to pay for it. I'll get you indicted!"

---

12. The name of the campaign also rather callously means "playing doubles," as in ping-pong.

Liu Changchun's old shortcoming—of not caring whom he offended—had riled Gu Zhuo. "I'd be perfectly happy if you went to
the County Committee and got me recalled! You think this job is a
piece of cake?"

Gu Zhuo later recalled something that Liu Changchun had said. "If
I can't topple Wang Shouxin, I'm not going to close my eyes when I
die!" Gu wondered how anyone could talk this way. Wasn't this
personal animosity? It never occurred to him to ask what was wrong
with a bit of personal animosity directed at the forces of evil. The
social forces represented by Wang Shouxin had completely destroyed
this man's family. Could anyone marvel that the White-Haired Girl
hated Huang Shiren?[13] But the Party members in the fuel company
not only felt no personal animosity toward Wang Shouxin—they
didn't even feel any "public" animosity toward her . . .

This, however, was not Comrade Gu Zhuo's fault. For many years
the commonly held view had been that the collective and the individual were separate and opposed. Personal wishes, feelings, and
inclinations, no matter how proper and reasonable, or even high-
minded, had all been trampled into the ground as "individualism" . . .

The various prejudices against Liu Changchun deterred the work
team from assiduously following up the important information he
gave them. Another piece of important information that turned up
was also ignored. This was a letter of August 28 written "to County
Party Secretary Guan in confidence" by the peasants of the Pine River
Brigade of the Raven River Commune. The letter raised nineteen
important questions about Wang Shouxin for the County Party Committee to consider. Each question was solidly backed by supporting
evidence. Moreover, the first of the nineteen points was, purely by
coincidence, the same matter that Liu Changchun had pointed out—
the "small-pit coal" surcharges that had provided Wang Shouxin her
opportunity for embezzlement. The letter clearly pointed out the existence of the problem and could have given the County Party Committee some concrete leads with which to begin their investigation.

But it seems the work team never saw this letter, or at least paid no
attention to it. How else could they have spent all of September and
October "so vexed we could not eat or sleep well" and still have failed

13. In the famous story "The White-Haired Girl," the heroine's hair turns prema-
turely white as a result of oppression by the landlord here referred to, Huang Shiren.

to determine whether or not Wang Shouxin was indeed guilty of corruption? And why would they have worried about the possibility of falsely accusing Wang Shouxin, making it "a terrible pity to have to reverse her verdict sometime in the future"? All they needed was a direct raid on her base at White Rock. Interrogations of Ma Zhanqing and Sun Xiyin would have provided the necessary breakthrough in the case.

The problem with the work team was the same as that with the County Party Committee. Both were divorced from the masses and therefore divorced from reality. The work team's attitude toward Zhao Yu, chief of the Commerce Section, shows the laughable proportions this problem could assume. It was obvious from the time they arrived on the scene that Zhao Yu ought to have been an important lead, so they went to him for information on Wang Shouxin. Yet the connection between Zhao Yu and Wang Shouxin was an open secret. Because of his public opposition of Tian Fengshan, Commissar Yang in 1969 had made Zhao Yu number-one man in the Party organization of the Commerce Bureau. Wang Shouxin had been his second-in-command. Zhao Yu had intercepted all the letters of accusation the masses had written about Wang Shouxin, neither investigating them nor questioning her. When Wang Shouxin pushed a large group of workers out of the fuel company, he gave her his backing. And it was also he who praised Wang Shouxin at a mass meeting called by the Commerce Bureau; she was "strict in the administration of her enterprise, ruthless in checking unhealthy trends, and correct when she revoked the licenses of certain drivers!"

In 1976, when Zhao Yu was doing political indoctrination at the Raven River Commune, he lived at the hostel of the White Rock Business Department. The commune's cadres, the workers at White Rock, and members of neighboring communes all rushed to him with exposés of the violent tyranny, the extravagant waste, the fraudulent pricing practices, the disruption of the economy, and other offenses perpetrated by Wang Shouxin and Ma Zhanqing. All of this Zhao Yu suppressed. "Don't try and mess with Old Lady Wang!" he threatened. "You'll only get yourselves into trouble!"

In 1977 there was an ideological clean-up of Party members in the Commerce Section. Shi Huailiang, as a worker in the pharmaceutical company, wrote four wall posters that were right on the mark in exposing Wang Shouxin. But Zhao Yu would not allow them to be posted.

When Liu Changchun put up his poster attacking Wang Shouxin, Zhao Yu, who could see that Liu did this at great risk, took pleasure in the prospect of Liu's suffering. "This guy Liu Changchun is quite a go-getter! The only one out of half a million people to speak out—he'll get what's coming to him sooner or later, just wait!" When Shi Huailiang wrote posters supporting Liu Changchun, Zhao Yu ordered the work team that was stationed at the pharmaceutical company to cause trouble for Shi Huailiang. More than ten struggle sessions of various sizes were held in an effort to have Shi Huailiang branded a counterrevolutionary.

It was precisely at the time Zhao Yu had ordered this persecution of Shi Huailiang that the Party work team at the fuel company came to him inquiring about Wang Shouxin's crimes. How absurd can you get?

But absurdities were everywhere. Here there was a work team sent to the fuel company by the Communist Party's County Committee, and at the same time cadres of the Communist Party were busy frustrating that work team as well as the whole Party Committee. While one of them was running to Wang Shouxin to warn her that she was the target of the campaign, another was concluding a pact with her to cover up each other's crimes. Yet a third was busily scheming with her about how best to evade the imminent attack. Let's look at a conversation between Wang Shouxin and the County Revolutionary Committee's chief of agriculture in August 1978, five days before the work team moved into the fuel company:

"I've come simply to warn you that a work team is on the way. You are the target; they're going to put you on the stand . . . Now, about that incriminating material I gave you . . . I want it back before it incriminates me."

"Impossible. Ours is a proper relationship . . . Can you arrange to have Liu XX be appointed leader of this work team?"

"I only handle agriculture; I have no say in such things."

"If you could arrange to have a woman sent, I could run her ragged, completely wear her out. Can't you figure out a way to have a woman sent?"

"Don't try to choose who'll be sent. Whomever they send will be tougher than Xun Hongjun, and that old geezer really gave me a hard time last year. Meng XX is all right, more stable . . . Liu Changchun once came to my house urging me to attack you, but I wouldn't."

Two days later, this fellow nevertheless went looking for Liu XX. "Do you have a work assignment?" he asked. "If not, come to the fuel company!"

Ah, connections! Such is the nature of those endlessly magical connections!

The final cracking of the case of Wang Shouxin was complex and exciting, especially in the way several hundred people were mobilized to track down and recover all the money. But I cannot use space here for all these interesting details, because there is a more important point that deserves our attention.

The more important point is that after Zhou Lu told the work team of his and Wang Shouxin's embezzlement, he begged the work team to protect him. "You have to be responsible for my safety," he told Gu Zhuo. "If she finds out I've told you everything, she'll move heaven and earth to get me killed. What if she comes to my door in the middle of the night to do me in—what am I going to do?"

In the case of Sun Xiyin, the work team had assigned guards to him beginning the very night he confessed. This had delighted him, for he also had feared that without such protection Wang Shouxin would kill him.

Liu Changchun's circumstances were somewhat different, but some well-intentioned people went out of their way to warn him, too. "Be careful when you go out after dark from now on," they said. "Wang Shouxin despises you. She'd part with a small fortune to see you dead."

Even reporters and investigators who came to look into the whole story of Wang Shouxin and Bin County had people come to them with warnings as they left. "When you come next time, you'd better look out for your personal safety. Don't take any comfort from the fact that Wang Shouxin has been locked up; the situation in Bin County is rather complicated."

The situation in Bin County was indeed complicated. And who can wonder that this is so? All ten of the people jailed in the case of Wang Shouxin were members of the Communist Party.

The former Bin County Party Committee Secretary, that so-called sly fox who married into Wang Shouxin's family, tried to conceal Wang Shouxin's embezzled funds for her. He also came up with a scheme for her. "Get yourself one of those giant earthen jars, put the money in the bottom, and cover it with something else. Then bury it as deep as possible . . ."

The "complications" did not end in Bin County. Wang Shouxin's eldest son, Liu Zhimin, was under investigation in Harbin by the Sungari River Prefectural Party Committee. His corruption and criminal activities had become quite obvious. Those "buddies" of his, who had arranged for him and his wife to get job transfers and who had removed incriminating material from his files (getting, of course, quite a reward for this) were still doing all they could to help him. Even when Liu Zhimin was "under surveillance," he wined and dined himself just as before; those charged with watching him helped him to while away the time by playing chess and poker with him. He could even hop into a limousine and ride to Acheng County, over thirty miles away, in order to conclude a mutual-protection pact with an accomplice . . .

The case of Wang Shouxin's corruption has been cracked. But how many of the social conditions that gave rise to this case have really changed? Isn't it true that Wang Shouxins of all shapes and sizes, in all corners of the land, are still in place, continuing to gnaw away at socialism, continuing to tear at the fabric of the Party, and continuing to evade punishment by the dictatorship of the proletariat?

People, be on guard! It is still too early to be celebrating victories . . .

August 1979, Shenyang City, Jilin Province

Author's postscript: For reasons that my readers can well understand, the names of certain characters in this piece have been changed.

WARNING

TRANSLATED BY MADELYN ROSS, WITH PERRY LINK

To attribute the catastrophe of the Cultural Revolution to one gang of only four people was a sophistry that worried many Chinese in the late 1970s. True, Lin Biao was eventually added to make five, and many people pointed discreetly to Mao Zedong as a sixth. After July 1980, Kang Sheng, a close advisor to the Gang of Four, could be named as a seventh. But the scale of such counting was still absurdly small. What about the tens of thousands of other "gang" followers? In the present story Liu Binyan addresses a "warning" to the Chinese people. Although the four departed souls in this story refer to specific people (the magnificent casket is apparently Kang Sheng's), they represent "spirits" that are very much alive. Yet, partly because Liu's message was a bit too bold, and partly because he had not been crystal clear about who the villains of his story were supposed to be, he and his publishers were themselves sternly warned, in spring 1980, for "Warning."—ED.

1

This was perhaps the most solemn place in the world. No noise, no movement. It looked as if a row of clocks, each having stopped at a certain time, never to run again, had been put out on display. Each item looked alike: a collection of containers all more or less of equal size, most made of wood and a few of marble. If one looked inside they were even more similar—just one heap of ashes after another. These were the last traces of what had once been living creatures, born and brought up on this earth, active for a few dozen years, and now in their final resting places.

Originally published in *Zuopin* (Guangzhou), no. 1, 1980.

Once, all of them had experienced both joy and sorrow, good and bad fortune. But what their final thoughts, feelings, and recollections were at the moment they closed their eyes for the last time and left the world of the living, is something that the photographs attached to the front of each container will never reveal.

I want to tell a story about a few of them who made their departures from life with smiles on their lips. Three of the containers were brightly colored carved marble, showing that the status of their owners had been out of the ordinary. These three men had once had a fierce desire for longevity, and thus, while alive, had daily consumed huge doses of tonics and elixirs that more than made up for the life juices that they had spent in pursuit of sensual pleasures. Now that they were dead, the excess of these potions could still be found inside their ashes, another fact that differentiated them from the crowd. Perhaps their desire for longevity had elicited God's sympathy, or perhaps some leftover potion was still having its effect—in any case a small amount of body heat from life still existed within their ashes. Thus, although their flesh and bones had disappeared, they still had not completely lost the feelings and spiritual attributes that had been so deeply rooted during their lifetimes.

While alive, all three had been consumed by one particular thought. Out of self-love and curiosity, mixed with a touch of terror, they had greatly wished to know how people would judge them after their deaths.

Few people visited this spot, for stepping into this other world naturally held little attraction for the living. But every time the sound of footsteps rang through this grand modern-day temple, the occupants of the three marble cinerary caskets became as excited as live wires. They would strain to catch the implication of every move made by a visitor from the living world outside. Yet they were always disappointed in the end, because no one ever spoke or expressed any feelings. Sometimes a visitor could be heard stopping in front of one of the containers of ashes, yet it was always difficult to ascertain whether he was paying homage to the dead or merely admiring the delicately carved decorative patterns on the marble. The sound of sighing from a visitor was always a tremendous comfort to the dead. They would savor it in their minds for days and nights on end, right up until the next visitor appeared.

Necessity is an extremely powerful force. If, out of necessity, mankind was able to create language, then why couldn't human remains that still preserved some body heat devise a way in which to communicate their feelings?

"They've completely forgotten us," the former general said one day.

"Perhaps it's better to be forgotten," said he who once was director of propaganda in a certain province as well as chief editor of its newspaper. The comment exhibited his cleverness.

"They can't forget. As long as my mines and factories still exist, they won't forget me," proclaimed the one who had been in charge of guiding the economy.

At this, the general, housed in his red marble room, and the director of propaganda, housed in his green marble room, both fell into a gloomy silence, nursing their wounded senses of self-respect and pride. There was no doubt that, compared to that man's, their own outstanding achievements would be easily forgotten. But the former newspaper and propaganda boss, being more quick-witted than the general, still had a comeback:

"What you say is true. But if anybody should happen to dig into the heavy costs you inflicted on people, then, old chap, I'm afraid your situation won't be so rosy. My newspaper always reported your accomplishments and covered up your mistakes. Remember the time you started construction of a factory, and ordered equipment, before you bothered to investigate subterranean conditions? When the project was over you discovered there was no electricity supply, either, so a few hundred thousand tons of steel got chucked into the sea . . . Ai, I still say it's best for us to be forgotten."

The economic leader lapsed into silence, and the three of them became lost in their own thoughts.

Time flowed on in the outside world, and changes took place. But the environment around the ash jars remained quiet and unchanging. The air around them seemed to have frozen into a solid mass similar to the marble vessels themselves.

One day, however, a puff of wind did blow into the vault. Judging from the sound of the footsteps, the visitors that day were different from any that had come before. They stopped in front of the three large marble jars, and even their breathing was audible. Then came a sound like an atom bomb, violently shaking these three unoffending souls in their tiny coffins.

"These scoundrels were all sworn followers of Lin Biao and the Gang of Four!"

The three souls had completely lost the last vestiges of their hearing ability. But their tactile sense told them that someone had spit on the pure and noble marble surfaces that sheltered them. Two days later they felt a heart-rending pain when someone used a knife to deface the photographs attached to the fronts of their jars. Soon they were each covered with a black cloth, which helped the three terrified souls to recover a modicum of calm. Then they began to ponder deeply and painstakingly on who this so-called Gang of Four might be, and what relationship they might have had with them . . .

Before too long the black cloths were removed. The three suddenly felt themselves swaying, and at the same time sensed the warmth of the living as it penetrated their marble jars. The three containers of ashes had been picked up. "Where are we going?" wondered the three souls, terrified. They could sense being carried from the moist dim vault out into the bright sunlight. Compared to the careful way they had been handled when initially carried from their memorial services into the vault, something was very different this time. The people who carried them now were either utterly careless or else deliberately displaying hostility and scorn. Under this rough handling, their once-human cinders were shaken to and fro until the order they had lain in these past years had been completely disturbed. This was very discomfiting.

Before the sun had had time to warm their marble surfaces, the motion suddenly stopped. Someone opened a rusty lock. Then, for the last and most violent time, the three were shaken up as they were thrown to the ground. The sound of human voices gradually died away, mingling with the sound of satisfied laughter.

2

Their world had been terribly cold and dreary to begin with, but now their grandiose marble garb made the three souls feel even colder. Cast onto the damp, dark ground, in a room that had long been abandoned, where neither sun nor human warmth ever penetrated, their cold loneliness can well be imagined.

But even all this could be endured, and gradually accepted. What really worried the three souls most was the question of safety. The desecration of their photographs had, at worst, been an affront to their dignity; compared to the crisis facing them now, this small matter was hardly worth mentioning. The question now was: would their misfortune end here or become even more serious in the future? Could the very worst happen? Could their stone coffins be smashed and their remains trampled upon and cast to the winds? Another worrisome problem was the fate of their families. One of the goals for which they had struggled throughout life had been to bring wealth and glory to their families. Wives, children, various relatives, assorted friends—all had basked in the benefits of being associated with them. Higher education, Party membership, job transferrals, promotions, salary raises, new housing, marital matches, trips abroad, and all other privileges available to Chinese were theirs. In addition, an inexhaustible supply of luxury products and nonmaterial pleasures, including many that for the common people were not only unattainable but downright unimaginable, used to arrive in a constant stream at their doorsteps. All of this sprang from the two or three magic syllables of their august names. Truly these names had glittered and shone like gold, attracting admiration and envy, symbolizing the pinnacle of power, glory, and wealth. When the three had made their eternal partings from their families, all of these privileges seemed solid, yea indestructible—for their sons, grandsons, and future generations. Using a few "connections," they could automatically obtain anything they might need. But now, in an instant, as their ashes fell from a top-class resting place into the dust, all the fruits of their fame were in danger: what if all were to be lost? That thought was bad enough. But even more fearful was the thought that the living standard of their entire clan might fall as low as that of ordinary people. No one was more familiar with the horrors of this possibility than the three souls. Tearful scenes of atrocious humiliations, scenes that they had not only witnessed personally but had taken an active hand in creating, were still fresh in their minds. Could this kind of fate now be awaiting their own families?

For many days the three souls remained completely quiet. Not long ago, they had found their greatest solace in those enchanting scenes and moods that they alone had once been privileged to enjoy. These recollections had helped them to forget temporarily the lonely and empty present. (Strangely enough, although they had long ago lost the flesh that is the seat of various desires, the memories of former satiations of their lust still brought them the most pleasant of sensations.) But ever since their fall into this place, these pleasant recollections had been countered by a simultaneous fear—that their families would be faced with wretched material conditions, be treated like dogs and pigs, constantly have insults hurled at them, and continually find the doors of opportunity now tightly closed against them . . .

Yet this uneasy silence did not last very long. One day, the noise of windows shattering frightened the three souls so terribly that they nearly jumped out of their marble containers. Next there came the noise of an angry mob. To the accompaniment of sardonic laughter, some rocks came flying in the direction of those three poor little marble caskets. There seemed to be a competition to see who could throw most accurately and strike home most frequently. If our friends the souls had had the power to protest, they certainly would have cried in pain and begged for mercy.

"Why flog a corpse?" the general grumbled to his companions when he couldn't stand it any more.

"This is simply too barbaric," added the director of propaganda. "And furthermore, it violates our ancient Chinese custom of passing final judgment on a man as the lid is laid on his coffin." He failed to consider that when his own cronies were at the summit of power, their barbarism toward the living had far exceeded stone-throwing. He also failed to consider that they themselves had long ago smashed the venerable tradition of leaving the deceased in peace.

Nevertheless, the stone-throwing episode actually brought the three souls a step closer to the world of the living, and thereby lessened somewhat their lonely isolation. It was now late autumn, when fierce autumn winds would sometimes howl through Beijing all night long. To the souls inside, this wind sounded like someone with a hard, thick broom mightily scraping away at all their marble surfaces. Sometimes they heard the sound of fallen leaves whipping at the window, and once in a while a few leaves would be blown through the broken glass to land on their marble covers. So in the midst of this cold loneliness they could take some comfort: they did after all have a few contacts with the outside world where they had once lived.

Fallen leaves and dust gradually built up a thin layer on the surfaces of their marble. It made the souls inside feel just a little warmer, just a little safer.

One of humanity's distinguishing features—hope—was something still not completely lost to the three souls. The economist based his hopes primarily on the case of an old leading cadre who, over twenty years, had gradually been restored from disfavor to a position of trust. His influence had grown steadily until he had reached the pinnacle of power. The economist recalled that this man's ashes had recently been delivered to the vault and had been set down not far from the three souls. But the fact that his cinerary casket had not later been thrown into this gloomy room with theirs seemed to show that this man hadn't been labeled a follower of the Gang of Four. Here, surely, was cause for hope. After so many years in the bureaucracy, the economist well knew that the greater a person's prestige, the more his "connections." This old cadre must have had some powerful protectors who had kept him from the same fate that had befallen the other three. Didn't this fact clearly suggest that the luck of the three, who had once been under the wing of this great figure, might take a turn for the better?

This thought was a turning point and a source of inspiration. For some days each of the souls, prancing to the music of the wind, returned to the world of his memories. They retraced the paths of their lives, carefully sorting out enemies from friends, as well as analyzing the ups and downs of those who were close to them. They had, of course, next to no energy left in their ashes for pondering such things. The last tiny sparks of energy that they did have they cherished immensely, and they used them to concentrate on the last twenty or so years. The people who had been toppled during these years had long been practically forgotten and were of no great interest now; but those who had risen, quite a few of whom had clawed their own ways to the top, could still be intermittently called to mind. Yes, there were quite a few of them. Surely they were all still living, and still wielding considerable power. Although they were not all fellow-conspirators, and some of them had even suffered extensively over the years, still they had all taken basically the same path as the three souls had, and everybody spoke a common language. Would they have changed easily—cast aside their hard-won gains and merrily altered their tune? Not very likely . . .

The spark of hope began to glow brighter.

3

The sound of a faint but thoroughly familiar woman's voice came from beyond the door, breaking the silence of this nonhuman world.

The sound of footsteps was followed by the wrenching of a rusty lock. The door opened.

The footsteps came closer. The woman sighed audibly, then spoke through tears.

"Can't you find a stool? You're not going to just put it on the ground like this, are you?"

The voice was terribly familiar, yet the souls couldn't quite remember who she was.

"You'll have to answer for this: I'm going to complain to the vice-chairman!"

With this sentence she had resumed her normal tone of voice and the three spirits guessed who it was almost at the same instant. "Well, if it isn't Sister Ts——!"

Before they had time to think further, a heavy casket—several times larger and heavier than their own resting homes—was plopped down in front of them.

It was a large cinerary casket of tortoise-shell marble. It was the largest, most exquisite, and most magnificent cinerary casket to date in the People's Republic of China. If one were to put the caskets of the other noble founders of the state next to this one, there would be no comparison, for the others were made only of wood, and each bore a simple photograph on its front—a small copy of the photo chosen to hang at the memorial service. But the casket of this grand personage had on its front a stately bronze relief sculpture of the man it contained. In comparison to the others, the new casket was like an imposing mountain peak next to a pale dirt mound. Its magnificence was marred, however, by the human excrement that had been smeared all over it, and by the irreverent markings that had been scratched all over its embellishments. Bronze is too soft a metal—the casket would surely have been made of alloyed steel had this day been foreseen.

The three souls, with the infallible political sense they had cultivated over many years, knew immediately who this person was. Great waves of emotion rolled through the stagnant pools of their remaining feelings. They were filled with shock and indignation, but at the same time a complex subconscious emotion was born in the bottoms of their jars. Here into their disgraced ranks had come a new member whose misfortune brought them the comfort of seeing others suffer. They were also grateful for the sense of cordiality and safety occasioned by the arrival of their superior and protector.

Over the years they had grown accustomed to being submissive and self-effacing before their superiors, and thus the three souls found themselves quite tongue-tied now, unable even to voice their greetings. Yet at the same time they feared seeming discourteous and thereby arousing the wrath of their superior, who had always been suspicious and cruel by nature. The rules of proper conduct in the living world would hold equally in the nether regions.

Their chief's perverse disposition had worsened after his death. This was due to the ceaseless pain that had spread to every cell of his body before he died. Every waking moment of his final years had been spent with violent headaches and horrifying hallucinations. Innumerable apparitions haunted him, attacking him one by one. They clutched at him and tore him to pieces, screaming of their unjust deaths. Among them were those who had died in the late 1920s and the 1930s because he had informed against them, betrayed them, or framed them. Then there were those who had died in the 1940s because of the forced confessions that he had planned and personally obtained, and those who were victims of the massive, nationwide witchhunts of the late 1950s. Even more numerous were those from the 1960s and 1970s—everyone from graying revolutionary veterans to young men and women in their prime, and even babies in their swaddling clothes. These unjustly persecuted spirits, smeared in blood, their hair in wild disarray, flew at him in droves before his wide-open eyes. If he closed his eyes they would still be there. He would almost explode from terror and the intense pain in his head, and of course sleep became utterly impossible. No sedative would work. Finally the doctor was driven to a last resort: he showed the leader movies, one after another, with no intermissions, from morning to night. The movie images helped somewhat to disperse the illusions before his eyes and in his mind, and succeeded in calming his nerves to the point where he could manage two or three hours of sleep per night. But upon waking he faced a new round of the interminable struggle. He resisted, he moaned, he screamed—sometimes for help, sometimes for mercy, sometimes madly bellowing like an insensible wild brute.

One who has held the power of executioner over the lives of a billion human beings, when finally faced with the phantoms of those who have died under his blade, finds himself trapped, and can only withdraw in helpless defeat . . .

Death ought to offer a kind of release; pleasures and pains alike should terminate when life does. But this exceptional figure could not shake off his exceptional destiny. Flames may have transformed his flesh and bones to cinders, but his pain, amazingly, had survived. Because he did not have a head anymore, the pain had migrated into each little carbon cinder that had once been part of his body.

The four souls passed many days in deep silence. The only sounds that broke through the deadly stillness of that vault were intermittent moans from the largest marble vessel. This moaning forced the other three souls to suppress some burning desires: first, to pay respects to their former chief in a manner appropriate to his station and to theirs; second, to comfort that extremely tormented soul in the hope of further ingratiating themselves. (This used to be one of their most developed skills, but by now they were losing their old touch.) They also had an irrepressible curiosity about the fate of their families and their reputations, and hoped that their wise leader might be able to shed some light on the subject.

Finally, the general—who of the three souls had been closest to the chief—mustered the courage to speak. He had barely uttered two words when an angry roar issued from the largest marble vessel:

"Shut up!"

A moment later, that familiar voice with its heavy Shandong accent began to speak, ever so slowly, in phrases that were interlaced with groans of pain:

"We must be patient . . . Let them forget, forget our existence. Now . . . there's only one, only one hope left . . . if those people . . . continue in the old ways . . . and move in our direction . . . that's our only . . . only hope."

His three companions knew his meaning perfectly, and the familiar image of his face floated before them: those gaunt cheeks, that cold, solemn glint in his eyes occasionally flashing out from behind his glasses . . .

From then on, the tomb was silent once again. Would history in the outside world move along according to the wishes of these ghosts? Or would more ash jars pile up in this forgotten place?

The autumn wind in Beijing was gusting fitfully, occasionally sending a withered yellow leaf through the broken glass and into the tomb, where in some small way it dispelled the deathly stillness . . .

November 1979, at the Literature and Art Conference

THE FIFTH MAN IN THE
OVERCOAT

TRANSLATED BY JOHN S. ROHSENOW,
WITH PERRY LINK

*The political relaxation of the late 1970s allowed the return to Chinese society of victims not only of the Cultural Revolution but of the 1957 Anti-Rightist Campaign as well. Intellectuals and former officials who had been in labor camps for as long as twenty years were reassigned to their original work units. Many literary works describe these "exonerations," but few penetrate beyond the happy appearances to explore the complexities that were inevitably involved. True to form, Liu Binyan stubbornly insists on penetrating, and in this thinly fictionalized account, refuses to whitewash what he finds.—*Ed.

1

Since the beginning of 1979, several hundred thousand people have come out into the sunshine from under the political shadows that have covered them for more than twenty years. Jin Daqing was one of these. But on his way out, he got caught in the shadowy twilight zone halfway between.

One day in March, this forty-five-year-old man, who wore a threadbare army surplus overcoat, walked up to a newly constructed office building beside the river. This building housed the newspaper on which he had worked for many years. As he noted the contrast between this elegant, eight-story building and the old one they had used twenty-three years ago, he smiled inwardly. It was a bitter smile. "The newspaper itself is still that one little sheet," he reflected. "But look how big the building has grown! The staff will be much bigger, too, of course . . ." His more than

Originally published in *Beijing wenyi,* no. 11, 1979.

twenty years of abnormal life had turned his whole manner of thinking and feeling inward. His face wore a permanent expression of apathy.

He didn't seriously consider that walking across that threshold a few seconds later would mark a new start in his life, or rather the resumption of his life where it had been interrupted more than twenty years earlier. He seemed, rather than nervous, to be absorbed in his own thoughts. This attitude led directly to his first mistake.

He knew that, of the twenty-seven persons who had left the newspaper office in 1957, he was the only one who was being allowed to return to work here. This was because, having been stripped of official status, he could be accepted for work only back at his former job. He was puzzled that the other twenty-three people who survived were not also allowed to return to their jobs. In terms of professional ability, political credentials, health, and experience, nearly all of them were qualified to do newspaper work. Some in fact had been middle-level administrators when they left. The things that puzzled him were many indeed.

He was near-sighted, and this, added to his habitual absorption in his own thoughts—which came from too many years in a place where it was unnecessary to greet other human beings—caused him not to notice the man walking toward him in the dimly lit corridor. This man, smiling broadly, had extended his hand long before he had drawn near and seemed not to take offense at Jin Daqing's social blunder. Jin did not recognize the man until he had been ushered inside the office of the political affairs department. There he saw Ho Qixiong, someone who had appeared countless times in his reflections on the past.[1]

"Welcome back! Our old comrade-in-arms returns to the battle-front of the news industry!" Ho Qixiong's sallow face was all

---

1. The personal names in this story suggest the characters of the people to whom they are attached. The surname of the central figure, *Jin*, means "Gold," while his personal name, *Daqing*, means "Great Clarity" or "Great Justness." The full name of *Ho Qixiong*, on the other hand, can be understood literally as "Where's His Heroism?" (Incidentally, we here use "Ho" to romanize the surname that actually should be "He" according to the *pinyin* romanization system. This is necessary to avoid confusion with the pronoun "he" at the beginnings of sentences.) The name Gu Tiancheng suggests one who relies on whatever Heaven deals him. The names of the women characters in the story all have positive connotations.

smiles, and his voice was full of warm feeling. At the same time, he never stopped scrutinizing Jin Daqing, who was seated at the opposite side of his desk.

Everything about the two men contrasted sharply. Ho Qixiong, who was short and small, wore a brand-new dark gray woollen suit. His face beamed. Jin Daqing—tall, strong, and serious—had by this time taken off his overcoat to reveal a plain cotton uniform that was faded blue in color and onto which patches had been sewn by the clumsy hand of a man. Ho Qixiong sat with his elbows on his desk, his fingers interlaced. He twirled his thumbs constantly as he spoke. Jin Daqing looked at Ho's hands, which were sallow and very soft. "He's never done physical labor," Jin silently observed. "I wonder if he's ever felt hunger pangs . . . probably hasn't."

At that moment Ho Qixiong was saying that, thanks to the Party Central Committee, under the leadership of Comrade Hua Guofeng, it appeared after initial reinvestigation that most of those on the newspaper staff who had been wrongly labeled "rightists" in 1957 could now be exonerated.[2] But we must be patient, as each person's case must be reverified and reconsidered on an item-by-item basis. And we may need to observe a nationwide quota policy. "Besides, we must of course review every individual's behavior over the last twenty years, mustn't we?" Jin Daqing glanced at Ho Qixiong. The weight of this last sentence was clear, even without reinforcement by the cold glitter of Ho's little eyes and the slant of his mouth. Who would do the "review" of everybody's "behavior" over the last twenty years? Ho Qixiong himself. Only the past twenty years and nothing else? Not likely. One's behavior now and in the future mattered more than the past. The crucial factor was how well one got along with Ho Qixiong.

As he waited for a response from Jin Daqing, Ho Qixiong kept weighing the case in his own mind: once this man is "exonerated," his Party membership will be restored, along with his grade-fourteen administrative rating—one grade higher than my own. With his years of seniority, plus his writing skill, he'll get an editorship at least. Ho Qixiong, of course, hadn't spent all these

---

2. In 1957 millions of Chinese were labeled "rightist" in a national campaign in which work units were required by a quota system to identify 5 percent of their personnel as rightists. After 1978 many of these arbitrary labels were finally removed.

years doing nothing. He had built up a network of connections in every conceivable direction. The only trouble was that he just didn't have it with the pen. Besides, Ho wondered, who knows how this man will treat me? After so much bad blood between us, how generous can I expect him to be? He knew he faced an acute dilemma. It behooved him to be as friendly toward Jin as possible in order to nullify any antagonism Jin might bear him; on the other hand, he mustn't be too soft. He must make Jin understand that his fate still rested mostly in his, Ho Qixiong's, hands. Ho was also aware that Jin Daqing was no pushover. It was his own stiff-necked resistance in 1957 that got him stripped of office and sent way out to the sticks. Thus Ho Qixiong felt a need both to bury the hatchet and to prolong the burying process as much as possible. Judging from the general drift of national policy and from the re-spect that Jin Daqing commanded within the newspaper office, it was obvious that once Jin was exonerated he would be promoted. Ten to one he would go higher than Ho himself.

The topic shifted to Jin Daqing's work assignment. "I can be pa-tient," Jin said. "I just want to get back to work, some regular nitty-gritty work, something like handling the letters in the public relations department." This took Ho Qixiong by surprise. He ex-amined Jin's countenance for some sign of whether Jin was sincere or merely pretending modesty in expectation of a better offer. But Jin remained stony-faced, his skin tanned and leathery—a condi-tion, thought Ho, that probably came from the ravages of so many years of wind and rain. (There was no way Ho could know that the social environment had been much more damaging than wind and rain.) A thought suddenly occurred to Ho: this guy has wised up. In the public relations department you don't have to write any-thing—it's a lot safer!

"We can handle that." Ho Qixiong's hands, which had been rest-ing on the desk all along, now pressed together and knocked lightly on the glass-covered desk top. A happy thought warmed his heart: the public relations department was well removed from the center of things. Advancement would be much slower there.

Looking at Ho Qixiong's unusually small eyes, a thought occurred to Jin Daqing: some people's eyes are several times larger than Ho's. Could the amount perceived by the eyes be proportional to their size? Immediately he found this idea too frivolous. But no sooner had he dismissed it than another leaden thought began to weigh on his mind. In 1957, this man was the one who had handed out the "rightist" labels. Now the same man is in charge of the "exonerations"!

So actually there was nothing strange in that weirdly absurd situation everyone was talking about the other day: the leader of a memorial service for a man who had been "persecuted to death" turned out to be the very person who had done the persecuting. Again and again Jin Daqing's large hands clutched the overcoat that lay across his lap. As he recalled all the well-meaning and fine comrades who one by one had fallen, he became aware of the tears that welled in his eyes.

Ho Qixiong noted the surge of emotion in Jin Daqing and made an inference: now he's going to bring up the salary question. Hmmm? Too shy to talk about it? Is he waiting for me to bring it up? Well and good: this will be a fine chance to show sympathy, show kindness, and also show him who's boss. Ho proceeded to remove his set smile, and—gazing at the cigarette he was turning in four fingers of two hands—slowly began to explain.

"The Party Committee knows you've had it rough all these years." Glancing at Jin Daqing he continued, "Times are hard, very hard. And back pay is impossible, quite impossible. Yet . . . we are old comrades, and just out of personal affection, if nothing else, I can't ignore your need. I still have a bit of clout around here . . . there ought to be some way we can make things up to you a bit . . ." Once again he glanced at Jin Daqing, who continued to show no reaction.

"Me? My own losses?" Jin Daqing's thoughts had been running in an entirely different direction. Using both hands he had slowly, steadily, been rolling up the worn-out old overcoat that lay in his lap. Finally it was tight as a knot. Then, still clutching the taut overcoat in his ten stubby fingers, Jin saw the faces of four people once again flash before his mind's eye. He was the fifth person to wear this overcoat . . .

At this point, if he followed the forms, he was supposed to say how grateful he was to the Party; how thankful for the concern of the local Party Committee; how the punishment he had received many years ago was at least partly deserved, and he himself hardly blameless; how he still today must strive diligently to reform his thoughts. He was also supposed to say something like this: Back in that year you, Comrade Ho Qixiong, selflessly and courageously stood up to defend the interests of the Party. Your denunciations and counterattacks all sprang from your love for the Party and for the socialist cause. Your denunciations of me at that time were just like your pardon of me today: both were entirely necessary, entirely correct. Who can say I've been thoroughly reformed, even today? I must beg you to give me more help and guidance in the future . . .

But he didn't say a word of it. He appeared to be distracted, and as he took his leave, merely rolled his eyes in Ho Qixiong's direction and weakly shook Ho's hand. He was depressed: four people! They all should have survived, as he did, to see this day—even if they had died the next . . . But I alone survived. Why me? Why? There were so many others better than me! . . .

There was another person—a person he did not need consciously to think about at that moment, or any other moment, because every drop of blood that coursed through his veins was in constant mourning for her. This was his wife. After keeping him company through twenty-three long, dark years, that uncommon woman had died a few days ago after a long illness . . .

Ho Qixiong interpreted Jin's sombre attitude quite incorrectly. Extinguishing his freshly lit cigarette in the ashtray, Ho mashed it fiercely and hardened his heart. "OK," he thought, "you want to fight, we'll fight. Just wait and see! . . ."

2

The public relations department, which in the fifties had been called the readers' correspondence department, was an auxiliary branch of the newspaper's editorial department. In the past, when the paper's mission had been to propagandize the ideas and goals that had been handed down from above, this department had had practically no function whatsoever. All of the many letters sent in by readers would just pile up in a corner or be handed over to some other office. (As often as not, the letters would end up in the hands of the very people they were complaining about.)

Jin Daqing threw himself wholeheartedly into his work with the readers' letters. One day a familiar name caught his attention: Jiang Zhenfang. He remembered a small, delicate young woman—perhaps a bit *too* kindhearted—who in the second year of her marriage had seen her husband labeled a "rightist." She had refused to save herself by divorcing him or, as the political slogan expressed it, "drawing a clear line." The letter now before him was from her younger sister. It asked for exoneration from a charge that made Jin jump in disbelief when he read it: "Whore. Bad element."

At first he imagined the worst. Had heavy economic burdens crushed her? Or, under so many pressures, had she abandoned herself in a fit of depression when her husband died? But after consulting the newspaper's personnel files, Jin began to doubt this line of reasoning. The other principal in this case of illicit relations was a notorious hatchet man at the newspaper, known popularly as "Fat Hands Dong." He was a Party member and had recently been promoted to chief of the automobile pool. Why had he chosen to confess his affair, without anyone informing on him, and without any pressure to confess? And why, after explaining everything, did he go around bragging as if this were something to be proud of? On top of all this, several of his witnesses seemed dubious.

It is perhaps normal that a case of "relations between the sexes" should arouse some interest. But why such a tumultuous uproar? Jiang Zhenfang had been paraded through the streets countless times, with a string of worn-out shoes, signifying adultery, hung around her neck.[3] Her own students cursed her, spat on her, beat her, smashed her windows, abused her children. This doubtlessly was all part of her being the wife of a rightist whom she refused to divorce. But even so it seemed like gross overkill.

In the end this woman went insane and entered an asylum. Her children had to be adopted by her younger sister.

One night when Fat Hands Dong was on duty at the automobile pool, Jin Daqing went to see him. Even before he knew why Jin had come, Dong was busy rattling off his "exploits" a mile a minute. Jin listened to him in silence, all the while gazing at Dong's ceaselessly gesticulating right hand.

"That palm isn't so big after all," mused Jin. "Amazing that it's been used to slap more than two hundred and forty people . . ."

Dong's account of things was so filled with crude language that he was hard to listen to, but some of the unspoken assumptions of his narrative were worth attending to. He repeatedly stressed details, as if afraid that people would not believe his confession. Two points he stressed in particular were that Jiang Zhenfang had a dark mole on her right breast and a scar from an operation on her abdomen. These

---

3. "Old Shoe" is a euphemism for "adulteress."

two points of information were what he had been spreading around for several years, and were what everyone considered to be the iron-clad proof of Jiang Zhenfang's guilt.

Jin Daqing could not devote all his energies to this one case. In the daytime he would read and reply to incoming letters, as well as receive official visitors to the newspaper. At night his ninety-five square feet of living space was usually packed with visitors. Most of these were people who had repeatedly appealed to the provincial authorities, or even the national authorities, for redress of various grievances. Most of their appeals had already been approved—some even by the provincial Party secretary himself—with orders that local authorities resolve the problems as soon as possible. But all this was to no avail. The last recourse was to descend upon Jin Daqing. With him there was no limit on time, as there was with the officials. He always listened attentively and tried to help each one find a way to solve his problem. Sometimes he even took care of their room and board. Where else could they find this kind of treatment?

Activities such as this could not escape notice for very long, however. Not only had Jin's "exoneration" not yet come through, but even if it had, a so-called exonerated rightist still had to be tested and observed. Even if he rejoined the Party he would be viewed as a borderline member, half in and half out, who could be kicked all the way out at any time. That's what some people meant by "letting the masses be judge of the labels."

When the first draft of Jin's "exoneration" document had been completed and was waiting only to be approved, it contained some favorable comments: "Some of Comrade Jin Daqing's suggestions in the fifties were worthy of adoption; the motives behind his suggestions were also benign," etc. But as luck would have it, the winds of orthodoxy were blowing hard this April,[4] calling into question the very basis of any and all "exoneration." The political department, moreover, had discovered that Jin's room was becoming a "rendez-vous for malcontents." Hence all the favorable comments in Jin's document were expunged and replaced by sentences like: "He may be reformable, but this is not to say he has not committed mistakes, some of which were severe," etc. His exoneration was shelved.

---

4. The oscillations between tightness and relaxation in Chinese social control had reached a relatively tight point in April 1979.

3

Jin Daqing made an appointment to go with Jiang Jinfang to see her sister in the insane asylum. He knew that one could not rely on information supplied by a mentally disturbed person. But he had to go just the same. Every night for weeks the image of his close friend Gu Tiancheng, who had died in his arms, kept appearing in his mind. He remembered what Gu's dying words had been.

This Gu Tiancheng, fives years his junior, had been a mild-mannered and timid person. How could he ever have been labeled a rightist? The question still preyed on Jin's mind. He knew only that Gu had been accused in 1958 during the "supplementary" phase of the Anti-Rightist campaign, and therefore his offense must have been minor. But he seemed from that time on to be stricken with paranoia. He seldom said anything in public. When he had to come out with even a single word, he would peer fearfully in every direction lest he bring more trouble upon himself.

He worked hard and conscientiously at the labor camp, but was naturally clumsy and often injured himself. When this happened he was fearful of being criticized for the injury, so he just endured the pain and pretended all was well. But his bed was right next to Jin Daqing's, and there were some things he couldn't hide from Jin. Once when he was stealing a glance at a photograph of his wife and children and suddenly discovered that Jin was looking at him, Gu laughed pathetically and buried his face in his bed quilt. Jin could hear his sighing beneath the quilt and could only heave a long sigh himself. Jin Daqing did not care for this kind of temperament but had to sympathize with Gu, and pity him.

Gu Tiancheng would occasionally ask him, very cautiously, "How long do you think it'll be before we're sent home?"

Who could say? But Jin Daqing could not bear to disappoint Gu, so he had to lie, saying things like, "I'd say pretty soon now," or "I don't see why they wouldn't send us home for a family reunion at Spring Festival." Gu was only too ready to believe such lies. When Jin Daqing saw Gu's face light up at his comforting words, he was upset to the verge of tears.

Autumn harvest at the camp took a long time. Even after it had turned bitterly cold, they had not finished gathering all the crops from the fields. Gu Tiancheng was approaching his third winter at camp, and his life had already become extremely difficult. During a rest period one afternoon he passed away. He was wearing that old army overcoat that had been passed on to him by the third person, and his hands clutched a steamed bun that had frozen hard as a rock. Jin Daqing embraced him and tried to warm him with his body and his breath. After what seemed like ages Gu barely opened his eyes, and called out his wife's name . . .

The person walking slowly toward him, supported by a nurse, looked more like a shadow than a human being. Could this be the beloved wife for whom Gu Tiancheng had longed day and night? A shiver ran down Jin Daqing's spine as he looked into the eyes of this walking shadow. They were nothing but two empty hollows, two dry wells. Jiang Zhenfang simply sat down and stared blankly, first at her younger sister, then at Jin Daqing. The sister took her hand and wept. The tears fell upon that same hand. Staring at the yellowed parchment of her face, Jin realized that the only traces of life still left on it were those two black hollows that had once radiated love and borne joy and fulfillment. He could not help recalling Gu Tiancheng and the photograph that Gu had treasured as his own life. "If only the departed knew . . .," as they say. No! It was better that Gu Tiancheng had never known. The only question was, should Jin now show to her the picture of Gu that he had kept?

Jiang Zhenfang turned around and looked at him coldly and suspiciously. When she did so, her younger sister leaned forward and spoke directly into her ear, pronouncing each syllable with great care: "He—was—with—Gu—Tian—cheng, he—was—with—Gu . . . "

Jin Daqing could see the patient's expression soften, and decided to hand over his enlarged photo of Gu.

The patient took the picture and studied it from top to bottom. All of a sudden a heart-rending cry of anguish shook Jin Daqing to the depths of his being. With wide eyes fixed on him and both hands outstretched, Jiang Zhenfang shouted at the top of her voice, "I want him! I want him! Give him back to me! . . . " Jin Daqing retreated across the room as Jiang Jinfang came forward to restrain her sister. Some nurses rushed over as well. Pushing the patient back and holding her up at the same time, they took her away.

As they walked back from the hospital, both Jin Daqing and Jiang Jinfang were so upset that neither spoke for a long time. When they reached Jiang's house, Jin stopped and said to her: "You must try to recall your sister's habits . . . Did she go to a public bathhouse? Could anyone, male or female, have ever seen her body? . . . Also try to find out if she ever wrote anything during her lucid intervals."

He seemed to detect in Jiang Jinfang's eyes an element of bewilderment and fear. Then, as they shook hands to say good-bye, he looked at her solemnly: "This whole thing may get messy, and you and I may get dragged into it. But times are better now, don't forget. Besides, you can rest assured that I will take the responsibility—all of it. But it'll still take some courage from you, of course." As he began to leave, he turned back to drive his point home. "Remember," he said, "This isn't just for your sister. There are so many others like her!"

4

Jiang Zhenfang's mournful cry echoed in Jin Daqing's ears for a long time. It rang as an urgent appeal as well as a wordless accusation. It also seemed to pose a mammoth question: Why?

He had long felt the injustice done to women in China. When a man was purged there always had to be some evidence, at least. And regardless of whether this evidence was true or false, the most it could bring would be political downfall. Furthermore, if the truth came out some day, a man could still look foward to a comeback. But women were different. All you needed was some rumor to spread, based on straws in the wind, or on plainly nothing at all, that Ms. Comrade So-and-so was you-know-what with you-know-whom, and that was curtains for the woman. At best, there would be a big brouhaha on the rumor mill; at worst, conjugal strife and divorce. It could even mean public scorn *for life*. Try to explain? How could you begin? Even if you could prove your innocence, the rumors had the case on record differently. Your reputation was shot. Would you be able to go explain yourself in person to each and every individual who knew you?

Jin felt there had to be a connection between the cruel fate of Gu Tiancheng and that of his wife, Jiang Zhenfang. Gu himself had said that in 1957 he never uttered or wrote so much as one politically incorrect word. Yet the so-called Party leadership decided that he was an anti-Party anti-socialist right-wing element. At first he had resisted this charge, but later he saw that resistance was futile. He and his wife wept for two nights before he signed a confession. This signing also came about as a result of persuasion by the "leadership," who advised that a perfunctory admission of guilt would allow the matter to blow over. How could he have known that he would still have to bear the "rightist" label, still have to be banished, still have to . . .

Jin Daqing sent Jiang Jinfang to the Bureau of Education to request, in her capacity as family of the deceased, a record of the official verdict on Gu Tiancheng that had been delivered in 1957. He was shocked to discover that no such verdict had ever existed, still less been approved by any level of district or municipal authority. This meant that Gu Tiancheng had never been a "rightist" at all! Heaven only knows whether fate has ever treated any person, or any family, as flippantly as this. The man at the Bureau of Education was impeccably polite as he informed Jiang Jinfang that, because Gu had never been a "rightist," therefore he could not be "exonerated." Jiang Jinfang protested, detailing the tragedy of this couple over more than twenty years . . . But the man only threw his hands in the air in helplessness. "What do you want *us* to do? You shouldn't have come here. You should have gone to . . . ah . . ." Indeed. Whom to ask? Where to appeal?

Yet Jiang Jinfang's visit to the Education Bureau was not a total loss. Out of sympathy, the people there went to Gu Tiancheng's file and found for her the incomplete record of a meeting that contained the sole piece of evidence against Gu Tiancheng. When he saw this Jin Daqing was beside himself with rage. The messy handwriting was barely legible. But there was no doubt about it: Gu Tiancheng's fate had been sealed by the convener of the meeting, Ho Qixiong. Ho had been schoolmaster and Party secretary of the high school where Gu Tiancheng and Jiang Zhenfang were teaching. The record read as follows:

> Schoolmaster Ho: You may have *done* nothing wrong, but we still can look at what you say. If you don't say anything we can consider your thoughts. And how do we know your thoughts, if you don't say anything? This can be judged from outward appearances. In all these meetings we have held since 1956, you have said less than anyone. And with a background like yours, you almost *have* to have certain dissatisfactions with the Party and with socialism. How could we expect you to be pure? You can't possibly be. Yet you keep quiet, you won't come clean.
>
> OK, everybody, just take a look at what the problem is here. This is even worse, even more dangerous, than those who are willing to expose their erroneous ideas, and who are courageous enough to un-

burden their hearts to the Party. This man is set against the Party in the
deepest recesses of his mind. If this isn't the most dangerous, most
vicious form of anti-Party anti-socialist behavior, then what is it?

Reading this record seemed to bring a flash of light to Jin Daqing's
mind, clarifying for him several things he had previously been unable
to piece together.

5

It was now early May. Those political winds which blew counter to
the liberal spirit of the Third Party Plenum were at their height.[5] No
one, probably, was more alert to this shift than people at the newspaper. Editors rushed around to revise plans, rearrange layouts, solicit new manuscripts. Writers tried to recall manuscripts they had
already submitted, or—badgered by panic-stricken families—to sub-
mit quick recantations of those articles. Readers, on the other hand,
were bewildered. They wondered what kind of major upset had suddenly befallen this country of theirs. All the slogans like "Liberate
your thought," "Break down the closed doors," etc., which only yesterday had been parroted all up and down the hierarchy, had in the
twinkling of an eye become flagrant heterodoxy. The remnants of the
Gang of Four popped up with new truculence: "What's this about
false charges and wrong verdicts? *We* are more wrongly accused than
anybody! How about some fair treatment for *us?*"

The political cold wind happened to come at the same time as Jin
Daqing's investigations. He felt doubly chilled all over. He could even
smell the poisonous vapors that were brewing inside the editorial
department specially for him. Any little thing he might do or say was
observed, noted down, and sent in secret to the hands of Ho Qixiong.
The number of times he had visited Jiang Jinfang's house; whom he
had received in that ninety-five-square-foot room of his; what he had
said there—all of this and more was reported in due course. Every
time he thought of this he smiled inwardly: They are on the decline.
Covert activity is all that is left to them.

It was common for Jin to encounter unnatural, menacing smiles in
the corridors of the editorial department. Sometimes he could hardly

---

5. The Third Plenary Session of the Eleventh Congress of the Communist Party of
China was held in December 1978. It marked the advent of many of Deng Xiaoping's
Western-leaning reforms, including "liberated thought" for writers and artists.

restrain himself from stopping people to ask what they were laughing at.

But when lying alone in bed in the dead of night, he again found repose. What did it all matter? The worst that could come of it would be a forced return to his same old life of the past twenty-three years. Now that his wife had gone to rest, he felt even less concerned about this possibility.

When he looked at the worn-out overcoat hanging on the wall—that old overcoat that had borne witness to so many tragedies—he cared even less about himself. He could stand above those brewing troubles that threatened his own safety and simply smile at them. For he was the fifth. He could well have been snuffed out long ago, in which case that yellowed overcoat would have changed hands once again. If he could now work to avert more such disasters, of what consequence was his own fate?

At times like this he would lose himself in reminiscences. He would remember those long winter nights, so cold and lonely, and be filled with complex emotions. Starting with the artist who was first to fall, he recalled their voices and expressions one by one, three men and one woman. When he got to the third, who was a woman comrade named Li Tao, his reminiscing suddenly broke off and his mind shot back to the present. A burst of inspiration had nearly made him sit up in bed. Li Tao had been Ho Qixiong's wife! That's right, back in 1957, when Ho had been transferred to the newspaper office, he and Li Tao had shared a correspondent's post. So how did Li Tao turn out to be a "rightist"? And who could have been her accuser?

6

There was a regular meeting of the newspaper's editorial department on May 27. But this meeting was unusual in that everyone was required to attend, even the chronically ill and the retired. The atmosphere could not have been more solemn, and was quite tense as well. Everyone knew something big was going to break.

The deputy secretary of the Party Committee, Mr. Ho Qixiong, was to chair the meeting. You could see in his expression a burning excitement beneath the solemn exterior. Little beads of sweat dotted his sallow brow. The eyes are the most candid part of the human body, and they betrayed his real mood: for him the meeting would be like celebrating a major holiday.

After the customary opening clichés, he got right to the point. He was lecturing in his own words, which is something he rarely did and which shows that on this occasion he was speaking straight from his own true feelings and political attitude.

". . . it is the same with the exoneration of rightists—we must not overdo it. We have recently seen a certain person who, though still not pardoned, has been sticking his tail in the air like something high and mighty, and again feeding us all that junk from 1957. What does this tell us? It tells us he has not reformed himself, and that we have also carried "the reversal of mistaken verdicts" too far. This person—flaunting both witnesses and material evidence—is attempting to help people reverse their verdicts. And what's the problem with that? It's just like 1957, when the rightists attacked the liquidation of counterrevolutionaries that had taken place in the early fifties. They said the liquidation was all a mistake, remember? Now we have just one more case of anti-Party, anti-socialist behavior. People are using the slogan 'Liberate thought' to attack the very foundations of the state."[6]

The speech stirred up a warm response from the audience. Several people were falling over themselves to express their agreement with Ho Qixiong, and even demanded the immediate launching of a new Anti-Rightist movement.

"I want to say a few words," came a voice from the back, as a lanky figure slowly unfolded himself into a standing position. The people in the front all peered backward curiously. It was none other than Jin Daqing, the main person under discussion.

"Of more than twenty rightists," Jin began, "I am the only one who has come back. And I haven't been exonerated, so it looks like the person we're talking about here is me. I want to address something very specific. As everyone knows, the high school teacher Jiang Zhenfang was once labeled a 'bad element.' Her family appealed, and asked for a reinvestigation. I did my own investigation, and I'd like to tell you what I found. Since our chairman has already raised this question, we must be sure to get to the bottom of it. First I'd like to ask Dong . . . I'm sorry, I can't remember his full name, everybody calls him Fat Hands Dong . . ."

---

6. Literally, ". . . to attack the four unmovables," (1) Party leadership, (2) the dictatorship of the proletariat, (3) Marxism-Leninism-Mao-Zedong-Thought, and (4) the socialist road.

"I object!" Fat Hands leapt to his feet, flailing his famous palms in the air. "This is a personal insult!" The room rocked with laughter.

"I'm sorry, I apologize," said Jin Daqing very earnestly, not imagining that this comment would only elicit new gales of laughter from the listeners. "I should call you Comrade Dong, and I'd like to ask Comrade Dong . . . no, first I have to explain to everybody why I am asking this question. The original evidence upon which Jiang Zhenfang was labeled a 'bad element' was supplied by . . . uh . . . *Comrade Dong*, and this evidence is what I'd like to ask about. Comrade Dong, you say you had illicit sexual relations with Jiang Zhenfang and cite two pieces of evidence to substantiate your claim. I want to ask you, since you say you have seen a black mole on her breast: just how big was that black mole? And was there one, or more than one?"

Fat Hands Dong was stunned. Struggling to maintain his composure, he tried to lead the discussion back to the agenda. "It seems to me inappropriate to discuss a subject of this nature at a meeting as serious as today's."

The crowd buzzed. One voice rose above the hubbub to shout out, "What's more serious than whether somebody is a 'bad element' or whether somebody has been wronged? Answer!"

A sudden hush, as everyone listened in intense curiosity to hear what Fat Hands Dong would say.

The chairman intervened in an attempt to break the siege. "Couldn't we postpone details such as this until . . ."

"No!" said Jin Daqing with firm bluntness. "You yourself raised this question just a moment ago. It was the question of whether or not I was trying to help bad elements reverse their verdicts. Remember? If we're going to do that we have to determine whether or not Jiang Zhenfang has indeed been a bad element. Comrade Dong was the primary witness, and the most important one, so of course we must listen to what he has to say."

He turned to face Fat Hands Dong. "I've given you my first question," he said. "My second question is this: you have said more than once that you've seen the scar on Jiang Zhenfang's abdomen. May we please know whether this scar was horizontal or vertical?"

A dead silence descended on the whole room. Three seconds passed. Five. The audience was growing restive. After approximately fifty seconds Fat Hands Dong finally mustered a reply: "As I recall, there was only one mole. As to its size . . . gee, how can I describe it? . . ." Again laughter from the listeners. Perspiration streamed from Fat Hands' face. On the question of the scar, he came out with another evasion and again incurred derisive laughter.

Stern and confident, Jin Daqing continued, "Wrong, Fat Hands Dong! You can't get off that easily. There are two moles on the breast of comrade Jiang Zhenfang. Look! Her sister recently did this sketch." He held up a piece of paper that showed two moles rather close together. The one on top covered about one square inch. The one below was smaller, about the size of a dime.

"As for that scar," Jin continued, "if you'd really seen it you'd have no trouble describing it. I respectfully request that the Party Committee look into Fat Hands Dong's crime of false accusation—and further, ascertain who was behind it . . ."

"Only the Party can decide such things," a voice interrupted. Then a tall man who had a few days' growth of beard stood up. This man was an important factional leader, and was currently in charge of a department. So his words had weight. "Today's meeting was originally a regular meeting of the Party, with non-Party members from the masses invited to participate. Recently Party Central has stressed the slogan 'The inner circle must come before the outer circle.' We must have no blurring of this borderline. I move that all non-Party people leave the room and all Party members stay behind to continue the meeting."

This put the listeners in some disarray. Rising to his feet, Ho Qixiong had already opened his mouth to proclaim the adoption of the suggestion to limit the meeting to Party members. But he was silenced as once more sonorous voice rang out: "How can you do *that?* You summoned these people here. Now, before the meeting's over, how can you say they don't belong here? Besides, *are* these issues purely internal Party matters? . . ."

7

The meeting had stirred up the whole newspaper staff from top to bottom, some two to three hundred people in all. Beginning in early June, the political winds in China once again shifted a bit, and people regained some of their boldness. Someone came forward with important news for Jin Daqing: Li Tao had been labeled a "rightist" in 1958 because of a few letters from Ho Qixiong informing on her. Li Tao had of course been kept in the dark about this. Ho Qixiong had even tried to persuade her to sign a guilty plea, promising that he would not divorce her. But Li Tao had consistently refused to sign. What good would it do?

As soon as the verdict on Li Tao had been handed down, and she was stripped of her Party membership, Ho Qixiong had divorced her. By that time such things were so common as to be taken for granted, and so this event did not arouse anyone's curiosity. Next Ho Qixiong tried to force Jiang Zhenfang to divorce her husband . . .

The reinvestigation of Jiang Zhenfang's case could have led to her exoneration and an alleviation of her illness. This hope was dashed when her younger sister Jiang Jinfang had another piece of very bad luck: her husband allowed himself to believe the vicious slander of some anonymous letters and came home quarreling a few times. He suspected her of infidelity, of hanky-panky with Jin Daqing. While Jin Daqing could shrug this off with a laugh, nothing so easy was possible for Jiang Jinfang. For her it was a new catastrophe on the coattails of the last. And there was no way Jin Daqing could try to explain to the husband—it just meant he couldn't see Jiang Jinfang anymore.

But Jin Daqing did learn a lesson from this. He came to realize that Ho Qixiong was not alone, and hence that he must expand the scope of his observations . . .

We cannot end without an epilogue on Jin Daqing's "exoneration" question. Ho Qixiong was adamant that the facts of each charge be carefully verified one by one; at the same time the political department, in charge of the investigation, became bitten with wanderlust. In early June two of their number were assigned to "outside investigations," which brought them first to Beijing, then to Sichuan, Yunnan, and Guangxi, and finally to Anhui via Shanghai. They had a great time at all the famous sights and didn't get back until mid-September. Jin Daqing, by some stroke of luck, finally did get exonerated—though not without qualification. A long "tail" would always drag behind him.

Meanwhile Ho Qixiong did fine. Since both Li Tao and Gu Tiancheng were posthumously exonerated, and their cases thereby closed, the bloodstains on Ho's hands were permanently whitewashed. Fat Hands Dong, who had benefited greatly from Ho Qixiong in matters of Party membership, promotion, and housing allocation, insisted that his framing of Jiang Zhenfang had been due solely to a personal grudge and had had nothing to do with anyone else. Hence Ho Qixiong to this day is pure as the driven snow. One hears now that he has even been nominated as a candidate for the Municipal Party Congress. His only worry is whether he can get enough votes, because—according to his highly developed sense of smell—the winds in China, not only in the province but in the whole country, are becoming less and less fragrant.

SOUND IS BETTER THAN SILENCE

TRANSLATED BY MICHAEL S. DUKE

The title of this piece of reportage, which carries in Chinese the connotation of "after all, sound is better than silence" (bijing yousheng sheng wusheng), is immediately recognizable as a dramatic reversal of the famous line "at that time, silence was more powerful than sound" (cishi wusheng sheng yousheng) from a Tang Dynasty poem by Bo Juyi (772–846) called "Song of the Pipa." Bo Juyi's line evokes the poignancy of pure silence when the sound of the pipa, a stringed instrument, ceases. The protagonist of Liu Binyan's piece, Zhou Jiajie, speaks in neither the sweet tones of a pipa nor the glass-shattering shrillness of die kleine Oskar in The Tin Drum *by Günter Grass, but he refuses to talk in the same way that Oskar refuses to grow during a twenty-year period in which his country and its leaders are pursuing ever more disastrous policies. In the end, his patience and his labors are rewarded; but clearly he will have to speak up loudly for what is right, because his former critics still hold powerful positions.—*TRANS.

The cacophony of gongs and drums, the earsplitting explosions of firecrackers, and the elated laughter and shouting of the populace filled every corner of the small county seat of Xinjin County in Sichuan Province. It seemed as though all 203,000 county residents had descended on the county seat on the same day, and everyone was quite obviously willing and able to express his emotions through the tumultuous noisemaking. Perhaps percussion instruments and even firecrackers were invented for precisely such occasions, when speaking and singing cannot fully express the intensity of people's emotions.

I really don't know at what time the people began to fear the sound

---

Originally published in *Liu Binyan baogaowenxue xuan* (Beijing: Beijing chubanshe, 1981).

of their own noisemaking and chose to remain silent . . . But during the New Year's Festival of 1980 in Sichuan everyone was talking and laughing to their hearts' content. During the New Year's Festivals of recent years, all of the well-wishing was essentially over by the fifth day of the first lunar month, but this year people were still visiting back and forth even after the fifteenth.[1]

In both the county seat and the commune, several groups of dragon and lion dancers burst forth on New Year's Day. The entire populace turned out to squeeze in around the wildly dancing dragons and lions and to catch a glimpse of which group would be the strongest and most daring in climbing up the tall pole to retrieve the prized red paper package hung there by a local shop or government office—this was an ancient custom, probably a rite of spring. Everywhere the older people could be heard to exclaim nostalgically, "Haven't seen this in over twenty years . . ."

It was an all too familiar refrain. Had not even the County Committee secretary and the commune and production brigade secretaries, describing the changes in the people's lives and production in 1979, remarked that "this hasn't happened here since 1957"? No question about it: in only one year the peasants' net income had increased an average of 40 percent, and town and country bank savings had increased more than 50 percent, not to mention a large increase in the rations of grain and edible oils. In what previous year had such good things ever happened?

For some thirteen hundred plus families, however, the greatest jubilation was not on that account. During many repeated campaigns since 1957, the heads of these households had been repeatedly branded as this or that sort of "bad element," and their families had had to suffer through ten to twenty gloomy and miserable years. This year marked the first time that these people could stand forth in the light of day and celebrate New Year's on an equal footing with their neighbors. Relatives and friends who had been forced to break off all relationships for ten to twenty years in order to "draw a clear line"[2]

---

1. The traditional Chinese Lunar New Year is celebrated from about the twenty-third of the twelfth month to the fifteenth of the first month of the new year. During the Cultural Revolution, the festival was greatly abbreviated or not held at all.

2. During the Cultural Revolution, the Chinese people were asked by the Communist Party to "draw a clear line" between themselves and any family member or friend suspected of political deviance.

were once again able to visit together. They were constantly repeating a single refrain: "We never thought we would see this day! . . ."

One person in the crowd received particular attention. The people crowded around the Fangxing Commune's lion-dancing troupe, continually pointed to a certain lion, and happily yet quietly exclaimed: "He's the one, he's the one, Zhou the Mute . . ."

I

In 1968, at the season for making grain deliveries to the state, an insignificant person from a small village in Sichuan's Xinjin County took sick. The illness was very strange: all he did was trip and fall, but it made him deaf and dumb.

The sick man's name was Zhou Jiajie, and he was a member of Production Brigade Number Eight of the Fangxing Commune. At that time, following the entire nation, the county seat was a flurry of activity—busily clearing out the class ranks.[3] As his family was helping this mute man along the central street in the county seat, they were met by a gaggle of people, among whom were some unfortunate ones done up with various colored streamers, clothes, and makeup to represent "class enemies." The former village elder was dressed up in a long Confucian robe, carried a water pipe, had a sword hung at his side, and was followed by a retinue of young village men. The getup of the KMT [Nationalist] army officers made them look as if they'd just stepped down from a movie screen. A "female spy" was so rouged up that she looked, a little too unrealistically, like a prostitute . . . The booming of gongs and drums, the chanting of slogans, and the repeated shouts of derision by the crowds who had gathered to join the fun and enjoy themselves laughing and yelling at that group of despicable enemies all blended together. The ink was not yet dry on their long banner, and Zhou Jiajie could only make out the last line, ". . . The struggle between the Chinese Communist Party and the Nationalist Party continues," as he was helped down a narrow little lane.

That was a particularly noisy era. The sounds of slogans, drums, speeches, arguments, laughter, sobbing, bloody battles, and explo-

---

3. Searching out "rightist elements" during the early years of the Cultural Revolution.

sions being emitted from the Chinese mainland fiercely shook the apathetic and unfeeling world of men as well as the dark chaotic universe, announcing the beginning of an unprecedented period in history. Not only was the Chinese nation to be wrenched off of its historical track, but the entire world was to be remade. The whole world concentrated its gaze upon this homeland of our ancient civilization and awaited with joyful expectation or fearful trepidation the advent of a great miracle.

Living in the midst of this world revolution, Zhou Jiajie must be considered most unfortunate! It was right then that he suddenly lost the ability to speak or hear . . .

He spent his meager savings on a month in the hospital, but his illness was not in the least improved. His family was most anxious and the villagers felt completely confused, but only Zhou Jiajie himself appeared quite unconcerned by his illness; and that was because he knew that his was an absolutely incurable malady. At that time, he was only worried about one thing: "I must never never let anyone find out that my deafness and dumbness are feigned . . ."

The autumn in West Sichuan had been quite lovely. All the grasses, trees, and various argicultural crops were greedily breathing in the sunshine in anticipation of the coming six-month-long season of darkness. The year's harvest had been fair, and one could more or less make it through the fall and winter; as for the coming year, in those days there was no reason to make any plans, and no way to carry them out even if one made them.

It was during that time that Zhou Jiajie took his son to deliver his grain allotment to the state. Father and son had each walked about seven miles carrying their load on shoulder poles. On the way home, their shoulders felt much lighter, and they should have been talking and laughing, but Xinqiang noticed that his father was frowning darkly without saying a word. Just as they were passing by a burial ground and the sky was already growing dark, Xinqiang suddenly heard the sound of something very heavy dropping on the ground. Turning back quickly, he saw that his father had fallen down by the side of a grave. The ten-year-old boy was scared to death. Later on the villagers brought a wooden door and carried the still unconscious Zhou Jiajie back home.

When Zhou Jiajie finally woke up it was already after midnight. He still had a slight headache. He tried to think back on how he had happened to fall down. If he had not had a head full of worries, had not been imagining all sorts of troubles as he walked along, he probably would not have taken such a tumble. A thought that had been pounding in his head constantly for the past few days now mercilessly drove out every other idea, even overriding the sporadic throbbing of his headache: "What am I going to do? They are going to beat me to death . . . Not even those leading cadres could escape . . . and that school principal lady . . ."

He had already seen many other people tied up and beaten, but this one he remembered with particular clarity. He knew her, that school principal lady. She had her hands tied behind her back and was hung there on a tree. Her attackers used a three-foot-long wooden club with a length of coarse rope tied to the end; the rope seemed to have been carefully soaked in water first. In the beginning the woman cried out sadly, but very quickly lost her breath and grew completely silent. Zhou Jiajie could see only the faint twitching of the twisted little finger of her right hand (either a birth defect or the remnant of a childhood accident); only that slight trembling of one limb showed that she was not yet dead. He had secretly wiped away his tears and quietly stolen away.

"They will force me to explain[4] everything. But I'm not an escaped landlord at all and I've never cheated anyone. Starving other people to death was never my mistake, but all of that is impossible to explain, and talking about it will only increase the weight of my crime. How *can* I explain it all? But if I don't explain myself, they'll beat me . . ."

This man of thirty-six years of age feared only two things: being humiliated or causing others humiliation; being beaten or beating others. He was too sensitive and could not bear to feel himself or others suffering either mental or physical pain. It was precisely this mortal weakness of his that made him quite ineligible to play the role of a hero of that age. If his heart had only been a little harder during those years, he would not have fallen into his present plight . . .

He felt a loud buzzing in his ears. Some people said that sort of a fall could bring on a stroke, one so bad a person might die or become

---

4. The term *jiaodai* is jargon for "explain" or "confess," depending on the immediate context; it frequently applies to persons accused of political crimes.

an invalid or even become deaf and dumb. "Mute?" Zhou Jiajie's heart beat faster: "If I really became mute, that would be fine. If I could not talk when they beat me and 'struggled'[5] against me, then they wouldn't beat me half to death . . ."

In this manner, then, this Chinese Communist Party member, this excellent rural cadre, this man who had given his entire youth to the great enterprise of socialist transformation, on this piece of land that he had watered with the sweat of his brow, in order to allow himself and others to go on living, was forced to make a final resolution to seal up his own mouth!

Early the next morning when his son Xinqiang called him for breakfast, he did not answer. Thinking he was still sleeping, his son came over and patted his blanket, but he still did not move. His son grew agitated and shouted at him, but he only opened his eyes slightly, shook his head, and made a gesture to indicate that he could neither hear nor speak. When his wife ran in and saw the way he looked, she was so anxious and afraid that she began to cry.

The villagers helped to take Zhou Jiajie to the county seat, but in the end they carried him back again without any appreciable change.

Feigning muteness was just a hasty expedient to deal with a pressing problem. When he "became" a mute, he did not even have time to think about what sorts of situations he would have to deal with once he "really was" a deaf mute. He had quietly contemplated that once this campaign was over he would just open his mouth and start talking again. But who could have imagined that the rape flowers would bloom and fade, fade and bloom again—that this particular campaign would last longer than the Anti-Japanese War?

Actually, when the Cultural Revolution began, Zhou Jiajie had long since become a "political corpse." In 1960 he was expelled from the Party, deprived of his position as production brigade branch secretary, and branded an escaped landlord and alien class element. In those days he worked very hard and was even given a model-commune-member evaluation, but he was still a nonentity as far as political and social life were concerned. Eight years as a political mute was no doubt very good preparation for actually "becoming" a complete mute later on.

He had originally thought that the storm of the Cultural Revolution

---

5. *Dou*, "struggle," is jargon for verbal political harassment.

would pass over such a political invalid as he was then. He never imagined that he would be unable to avoid trouble. The village Rebel Faction leader, Wang Quan, came to visit him, urged him to join their "organization," and promised, "We can settle your case." Zhou Jiajie knew very well what sort of a character Wang was and so he diplomatically declined his offer. Of course he hoped to get himself exonerated, and he never gave up hope that some day he could return to the Party ranks, but that was an internal Party matter that had nothing at all to do with the likes of Wang Quan!

A short while later, Zhou Jiajie went to market and saw a bulletin listing twenty targets of the class "purification" campaign. He immediately tensed up and an inauspicious premonition seized hold of his mind. Just as he expected, in a few days' time big character posters appeared reading, "Drag out the alien class element Zhou Jiajie!"

In 1960, when he had been expelled from the Party and branded an alien class element, Zhou Jiajie believed that that was the final blow. He thought that he had fallen to the lowest level of society. Who could have imagined that they would have to "continue the revolution"? This new attack made it impossible for him to express his hopes, desires, opinions, or feelings, or even to associate with other people.

This was not the end of his troubles, however; misfortune itself seemed to possess the ability to grow naturally. When you are forced to pretend to be deaf and dumb, you in fact leave yourself open to even greater calamity: if it is ever revealed that you are only pretending, then you will never be able to escape even greater punishment. That a class enemy like you could have the effrontery to escape from struggle and trick the revolutionary organization! Redoubled humiliation and heavier blows from revolutionary clubs might descend on Zhou Jiajie at any moment!

Zhou Jiajie could do nothing less than prepare himself thoroughly for whatever circumstances might arise at any time. Living among other people, he had to sever all natural relations with them. That was no easy task!

When he walked down the road and people approached him, he ignored them if he could; if not, he simply nodded his head. If he met a close acquaintance he could smile a little. That became Zhou Jiajie's only opportunity to smile. A smile in any other situation could give rise to suspicions that he had heard something.

Most frightening were sounds that came from behind; there was almost no way that he could guard against them. Once when he was cutting bamboo and a woman came up close behind him and gave a fierce shriek, Zhou Jiajie shuddered all over. The woman began to wonder: How could this deaf man hear my shout? Luckily, his nephew, Zhou Zhongci, was sitting beside him and spoke up, "How could that be?! I've tried it many times, he simply can't hear. When he moved just now it was only because he wanted to move." In that way the woman was just barely mollified.

While working in the fields together, people like to banter back and forth and come out with humorous quips. Everyone could laugh when this happened—everyone except Zhou Jiajie. Not only could he not laugh; even if his face twitched slightly or the expression in his eyes changed, he could be giving himself away!

Zhou Jiajie was not being overcautious. He had already heard people angrily exclaim many times, "He's faking pretty well all right, but if we dragged him down to a struggle session we'd see if he could talk or not!"

Sometimes Zhou Jiajie actually envied true deaf mutes. "I'd be a lot safer if I were really deaf!" Sure, he could close his eyes and not see, he could cease to sniff with his nose, and he could keep his mouth shut; but how could he stop up his ears? How could he hear something and yet have no reaction? Nevertheless, Zhou Jiajie knew in his heart that he had to succeed at this. He knew that his own ears had already changed from an indispensable organ of life into a dangerous threat, a tool that other people might use to harm him.

II

His new life was not completely without compensation. After he had broken off all associations with other people, he found that he had more time to think about himself and his past experiences. The one thing that he kept pondering over and over again was how he, Zhou Jiajie, had come to such a sad pass.

At Liberation the seventeen-year-old Zhou Jiajie was still in school, but from the time Land Reform began he was an activist. He led the way in setting up Mutual Aid Teams. When others chipped in one or two thousand square feet of land, he threw in a whole acre. And when the autumn harvest was counted up, his team had the highest productivity, with an average of thirteen hundred pounds more per acre than all the other teams—one acre produced over two tons of grain, a feat that was not to be repeated for more than twenty years. It created a sensation throughout the district and people came to the grain distribution station to learn from them, asking them to summarize their experiences. Young Zhou Jiajie's organizational skills and economic abilities became apparent that year.

In 1953 Zhou Jiajie joined the Youth League and the Communist Party. He was the first middle peasant Party member to be recruited by the rural Party branch office. Naturally, this could not have been without good reason.

Zhou Jiajie also led the way in organizing early Agricultural Producers' Cooperatives. When these were transformed into advanced APCs, his responsibilities increased, and his economic abilities were given even greater scope to develop. His cooperative organized a collective pig farm, a noodle factory, and an apiary, all of which were well administered and made a great deal of money, once again becoming the most outstanding enterprises in the district. Everyone said that Zhou Jiajie was the district elder's "big-headed hammer," and that was the simple truth.

How could he help becoming the district elder's "big-headed hammer"? For every campaign, mission, or important undertaking, the district leaders called upon Zhou Jiajie to strike the first blow; and he really could strike a resounding blow. All the Party had to do was put out an appeal and he, Zhou Jiajie, was certain to respond. Whenever he made promises or issued challenges to other cooperatives, he always had a very practical plan in mind and never made idle boasts or went off half-cocked.

It was really quite hard on Zhou Jiajie to continue to press forward as single-mindedly as he did. At that time his family consisted of his old father, a widowed sister-in-law, and his wife; he was the only able-bodied male laborer. But so much of his time was taken up just attending meetings! It was often three or four in the morning before the meetings let out. When he returned home, the cooperative members were already preparing to start work. His family always complained. With his strength he could easily make three or four thousand work points a year, but as a cadre he only received a four- or five-hundred-work-point subsidy. Besides that, he didn't really think about his own family; if the cooperative lacked for anything, he would often take it from his home and give it to them. One time the cooperative needed some lumber and Zhou Jiajie simply told them, "Cut down my willow trees; cut down my pine trees!" His old father was so angry when he saw him light the lamp at night that he yelled at him, "What the hell are you reading? Put out the lamp!" The old man felt that their family had already suffered enough losses and was unwilling to add lamp oil to the list.

The pressure from his family had occasionally given Zhou Jiajie second thoughts: "Maybe I'd do better not being a cadre, just working my farm instead . . . A lot of people have gotten rich these last few years." But then as soon as he considered that he was a Party member, considered that the local people trusted him and put the heavy responsibility for all of their property on his shoulders, and then remembered the commitment he had made to the Party and the local people—when he considered all of these things, his enthusiasm was rekindled and he began to work even harder.

That period seemed like a long, long time; it was actually no more than five short years, but what exciting years they were! Year by year life was improving right before one's eyes, and everyone worked with great enthusiasm. In Party meetings one felt just like a child beside its mother; you could say anything you thought and never worry about offending the leadership. When the state monopoly of purchasing and selling began, the leadership had criticized Zhou Jiajie as part of their effort to fulfill the state purchasing quota; but it was only a gentle reprimand and nothing came of it later.

Actually, Zhou Jiajie had been wronged even in that situation. When the state monopoly began in 1953, he made a careful estimate and decided to sell 1,650 pounds of his own grain, no small amount at that time. But the "work cadre" Han who was sent out from the county seat tapped his pencil on that 1,650 pound figure, mulled it over a few minutes, and then sort of mumbled out loud, "1,650, that's a little short, isn't it?" When Zhou Jiajie heard that, he felt hurt and immediately blurted out, "Then I'll sell 2,200 pounds!" as if he had really done something to let the Party down. In his eyes everyone sent down from the leadership ranks was the embodiment of the Party itself. If the Party felt the figure was too small, it must be because the revolution needed the grain. One result of his action was that his family complained bitterly to him. They had to live on short rations for several months that year.

Everyone says that 1958 was a turning point, but actually, many things were beginning to happen much earlier; it was just that no one really understood them.

Nineteen fifty-eight was certainly an historically unprecedented year. For a few months a carnival atmosphere prevailed. And how could people help being ecstatic? Suddenly they discovered that the communism they had thought was still in the distant future was right there before their very eyes! Everyone, even the Chinese Communist rural cadres so long noted for their extreme practicality, was caught up in the foolish intoxication of those days. Even Zhou Jiajie was slightly influenced in that direction.

Everything in those days had to break with convention— immediately, as quickly as possible, and as thoroughly as possible. Take Party meetings, for example. This most familiar activity of rural cadres took on a new form that year. Party meetings themselves were regarded as a magnificent method of "production." You see, every time a meeting was held, the per-acre grain production could shoot up several times. This kind of labor should not be slighted; it wasn't easy. The leadership had to apply great pressure; the grassroots cadres had to squeeze for all they were worth; then more pressure; then squeeze again . . . over and over until the production figure reached unprecedented levels and could be gloriously announced— say ten tons or even thirty tons per acre—and then their great work was accomplished and the meeting could be adjourned. Until they came up with a "big increase in production," the grassroots cadres could not even dream of leaving the meeting.

After a meeting in those days (when a meeting occupied many consecutive nights), even a strong young man in his twenties like Zhou Jiajie staggered down the road on the way home. When he got back to the production brigade at two or three in the morning, he still had to wake up all those commune members who had just closed their eyes after the nighttime struggle for production in order to an- nounce where the next day's ceremonial "battle in the fields" was to take place, how all the tools and implements were to be arranged, etc. By the time everything was arranged properly, it was time to go to work again.

Zhou Jiajie's commitment to communism was beyond question; he wished that it could be realized tomorrow morning. With his great faith in the Party, he carried out every directive with his usual alacrity; but there was one thing that was very different from previous years: he often felt a struggle going on in his mind. There was one voice that accused him of being too conservative, backward, and unable to overcome superstition. This was an extremely gruff and frightening voice, though somewhat abstract. Another voice kept saying other things: The crops are sown too close together, aren't they? The production target is set too high, isn't it? We're going too fast, aren't we? Is this right? Can it be done? . . . This voice was rather weak and timid, but it accorded with Zhou Jiajie's experience and the things he understood so well. For some reason, the more the conflict continued, the more he began to listen to the second voice.

At first, when the leadership asked him to do something, no matter what it was, he would carry it out, just as in the past; but gradually his faith in them weakened. Finally, he began to hold back a little and even to resist them in varying degrees. The orders he carried out were to collectivize hogs, to collectivize furniture and tools, to abandon work points, and to take meals in big communal mess halls. When the leadership went on to promise that everyone would soon move into "big buildings," each with an upstairs and a downstairs, electric lights, and telephones, he completely approved in his heart, but at the same time he felt somewhat confused. Where were the bricks and lumber to come from? When the order was issued to tear down the old houses, he couldn't do it. Although the houses were not his, he knew full well how much bamboo, wood, and labor it had taken to build them. He just couldn't do it. He couldn't help feeling skeptical: Why all this haste? If we tear down our old houses before we have any way to build new ones, where are we going to live? But he had to tear them down—it was a question of his attitude toward the "Three Red Banners."[6] Zhou Jiajie had to be resourceful; he chose only the oldest and most dilapidated houses for destruction. After he did that for a while, his conscience began to trouble him: was he not merely feigning compliance with the leadership? He should rightly report his own opinion and the actual conditions to the Party.

Recalling that period of history ten years later [1968 recalling 1958], Zhou Jiajie was much more aware of what had happened. The seeds

---

6. The "Three Red Banners" were the General Line for Socialist Construction, the Great Leap Forward, and the People's Communes.

of his present calamity had been sown mostly at that time. His thinking had been, and still was, too "conservative." He could not break the habit of "seeking truth from facts."[7]

At the district meeting called to report production figures, Zhou Jiajie screwed up his courage and reported, "Our commune production this year will average 3300 pounds per acre." Before he'd even finished speaking, he could see that Party Secretary Cai's expression had changed abruptly. His heart sank and he knew he'd never get away with it. As expected, Secretary Cai pounded the table. Not long ago a county investigating team had discovered that Zhou Jiajie's commune was not planting the rice sprouts close enough together. They had criticized Zhou on the spot and made things embarrassing for District Branch Secretary Cai. And now Zhou Jiajie was reporting this disappointing figure; no wonder Secretary Cai was angry. He bellowed out: "Zhou Jiajie, you must be sleeping! Commune Number 21 has already reported six and a half tons per acre, and a progressive commune like yours comes up with less than two; how can that be?" Zhou Jiajie bowed his head and remained silent. Of course he knew if he reported six and a half tons he would win a prize—he could take home a brand-new bicycle and make a good impression on the leadership. But what would they do at autumn harvest time? He was responsible for over 130 families, with more than 500 mouths to feed; after the state grain purchases, could he ask them all to go hungry? . . . Later on, a female cadre from the county office told him: "You'd better report at least five tons; otherwise you'll never pass inspection." Zhou Jiajie hardened himself as much as he could: All right, if I have to report, I'll report three tons. How could he have known that the next day the ante would skyrocket again? One commune secretary actually reported a figure of thirty-three tons per acre! Zhou Jiajie once more became a midget. County Work Organization Director Zhang was extremely dissatisfied and kept staring at Zhou Jiajie. Not long after that meeting, the rumors began to fly: Zhou Jiajie used to be an outstanding district worker, and always understood the leadership's plans very quickly, but now he's no good: there's no question that his feelings about the Great Leap Forward are wrong. Zhou Jiajie did not know that he was already being closely watched.

---

7. The pragmatic slogan associated with Deng Xiaoping and the present Chinese Communist Party leadership.

There certainly were many "new things"[8] that year. For the previous few years Zhou Jiajie had always taken the lead in developing "new things," but that year he could no longer do it. He could no longer lead the way in burning up the people's firewood in order to scorch the earth and carry out full scale "militarization," in ordering old women to perform morning calisthenics and running, in making everyone sleep in their fields at night, in wasting perfectly good trees in order to make "wooden tracks" and carry out full-scale "vehicularization," in eliminating work points and changing to a fixed-wage system,[9] and even in smashing all private household cooking utensils in order to secure the "changeover to communal eating without any thought of turning back."

Zhou Jiajie felt extremely perplexed. Wouldn't he be happy to enter into communism tomorrow? That was why he joined the Party in the first place, but now he felt a certain uneasiness and suspicion. His keen insight into agricultural problems, handed down to him by generations of his ancestors, automatically made him respond negatively to those formalistic work methods that did not pay close attention to practical results: using up so much firewood to scorch the earth, tearing down the commune members' walls in order to fertilize the fields,[10] cutting down perfectly good bamboo for use in the mess-hall cooking fires . . . was all that worth the effort? What were they trying to accomplish? Why did they want the commune members to smash up their perfectly good pans and dishes? Were they supposed to eat out of their hats in the mess halls?

His greatest anxiety concerned the food supply. As a leader of mutual aid teams and agricultural cooperatives for several years, he had always had a certain balance sheet in mind: one acre can produce so much grain, one person can eat so much, and the state will purchase so much. Therefore, no matter how much the leadership kept on shouting, "What do we do if there's a surplus of food? Loosen your belts and eat up; build up your enthusiasm and produce," he continued to separate the food rations into three parts and ordered

---

8. The phrase "new things" or "socialist new things" (*shehuizhuyi xinshi*) was jargon for all sorts of social and economic innovations pushed by the Party during the Great Leap Forward and the Cultural Revolution.

9. This system destroyed incentives by paying people the same wages regardless of what they achieved.

10. The straw that peasants mixed with mud in building walls could, after some decomposition, be used as fertilizer.

the mess hall to supply reasonably measured amounts. That only made the commune leadership angry again, and they sent down an order abolishing measured amounts. What could he do? Zhou Jiajie watched the commune members consume more than two pounds of grain per person each day, and he grew terribly anxious: when the autumn passed, what would they eat in the spring? A short while later it was time to pay the commune salaries. Where was the money to come from? The leadership sent down an order: cut down the commune members' bamboo and sell it in the marketplace! When this was done there was barely enough for each person to receive $1.30. The "communal mess system" had been in effect only two months, but the food ration was already exhausted. The best they could do was return to the system of rationing. By this time each person was to receive only three and a half ounces [two Chinese *liang*] per meal. But even these rations were not available. Originally over seventeen acres of red potatoes had been planted, but Secretary Cai did not have them harvested. He said, "Don't be so short-sighted; there's more rice than we can eat, so who wants those damn red potatoes?" But Zhou Jiajie continued to have some people secretly dig up a few and store them; in that way he could barely fulfill those "three and a half ounce" rations.

More and more things grew incomprehensible to Zhou Jiajie, and he became increasingly depressed. His production brigade was located at a road that everyone had to use to go from the commune center to all of the other production brigades. Consequently the leadership asked them to give a particularly large number of "performances"—night tilling, close planting, deep plowing . . . Even Zhou Jiajie, a grassroots cadre who had always been a devout believer in the leadership and in every directive they issued, finally arrived at a day when he simply could not take it.

One day another investigation team arrived from County Central. Commune Secretary Cai ordered Zhou Jiajie to take the deep-plowing team to the east side of the village to perform and then, after the investigation team had passed, to rush his people to the west side of the village so that the investigators could witness the performance again on their way back to the commune center. Before the commune official had finished conveying the order, Zhou Jiajie lost his temper and yelled at him, "What are you trying to do? Treat us like actors? We've got water buffaloes and plows and there are so many ditches to cross over—you know how much work it is to move from one side to the other? . . . You tell Secretary Cai we're not going to do it!"

A short time later, Zhou Jiajie lost his position as production brigade branch secretary and was sent to be a substitute principal at the production brigade's agricultural middle school.

III

By the beginning of 1959, a famine had already developed. Zhou Jiajie's Fifth Brigade could sell to the state only half the grain that they had been obliged to promise. This was hardly surprising, since, according to the inflated quotas, Fangxing Commune was supposed to complete a grain sale to the state of 4.4 million pounds. But that year's harvest amounted to a total of just over that amount—where were they to find all the "surplus" grain? According to the false production reports there was still supposed to be more than four million pounds in the people's hands even after subtracting their grain rations. If you said there was no more grain, would the peasants believe you? Thus the County Committee issued an urgent order: all of the grain currently stored at the various production brigades could not be moved, but must be gathered up and put into "people's granaries" in preparation for sale to the state.

What about seed grains then? There were no seed grains. The seedling fields had long since been made ready and were only waiting for the seedlings. Mosses and weeds began to flourish there, but there were still no paddies planted with seedlings . . .

In the last month of that year a struggle meeting was called by the production brigade to criticize and denounce Zhou Jiajie. The meeting was run personally by Ji Weishi, the former Party committee secretary of Dengshuang Commune. As it turned out, Secretary Cai of Fangxing Commune, the one who had believed Zhou Jiajie was too "right," had himself already been declared guilty of "rightist deviation" and deprived of his office. As an expert in class struggle, Ji Weishi had been sent down by the County Committee to rectify this backward commune. He brought along a great troop of people and took over the power and authority of several production brigade branch secretaries and bookkeepers.

"Zhou———Jia———jie———," Secretary Ji poured as much hatred as possible into his enunciation of those three syllables. His booming voice, which belied his short stature, immediately quieted the entire hall and established his authority and status as the embodiment of the Party: "This evil person who has wormed his way into our Party ranks is trying with all his might to topple our great, glorious, and correct Communist Party and ruin the work of socialist construction. We call on him now to confess to the criminal activities he has carried out from October of this year until this moment, activities intended to oppose the 'Three Red Banners,' to topple the Eighth Production Brigade, and to injure the welfare of poor and lower-middle peasants!"

That was the first time that the twenty-eight-year-old Zhou Jiajie had stood in the accused's box. He was firmly convinced of his innocence and integrity, but the atmosphere of the meeting and Secretary Ji's tone made him feel unusually nervous. He was willing to admit his mistakes, even those mistakes that it was not really his responsibility to admit, but there was no way that he could accept the charge of being an "evil person" and confess to "criminal activities." While he was still trying to figure out just how to respond to such accusations, the agenda was advanced to the stage of "denunciation by the commune masses." He realized quite sadly: "I've been made a landlord!"

It seemed as if everything had been carefully prepared beforehand. The bookkeeper stood up and "confessed" that twenty dollars of the hundred and thirty dollars he personally had embezzled had been taken by Zhou Jiajie. Zhou Jiajie remembered very clearly that this bookkeeper had lent him twenty dollars two months ago when they went to market together. He had asked him specifically if it was public or personal money. The bookkeeper said it was his own money, and only then had Zhou borrowed it, saying very clearly, "I'll pay you back as soon as I sell my hog." Another person stood up to accuse him: "What do you mean only twenty dollars? The cooperative's noodle factory was ruined by him alone with several thousand dollars going into his own pockets; where else would he get the money to dress so well?" Zhou Jiajie laughed to himself: that would be easy to clear up. All the money had gone to buy fertilizer. It hadn't been as much as that, either. Yet another commune member stood up and said that Zhou Jiajie always sat his ass on the side of the landlords. Once he had borrowed a hoe from a landlord, a broken hoe at that, and Zhou Jiajie had made him guarantee compensation to the landlord.

All that was only a prologue. The play proper was just about to unfold . . .

Wang Quan—who would become a rebel faction leader seven years later—volunteered to reveal Zhou Jiajie's family history in order to supply Secretary Ji's needs. He also incited a crowd of people to join in his accusations. At that moment he jumped to his feet and shouted: "Zhou Jiajie himself is nothing more than a dyed-in-the-wool landlord element!"

This was something one could not afford to be vague about. Zhou Jiajie knew very well the weight of that word "landlord." He wanted to explain before the district people that there must have been some mistake. At the time of the land reform, his family owned only two and two-thirds acres of fourth-class land, a little over a third of an acre per person, which was less than the average amount per person in the village as a whole.

"Tell us, what relation do you have to Zhou Sanma's wife?" Wang Quan asked accusingly.

Zhou Sanma's wife? She was pretty famous. Right, she was Zhou Jiajie's great-grandmother. Zhou Jiajie began to explain that the family fortune completely declined during his grandfather's generation.

Before he could even finish speaking, a loud "thump" resounded through the hall as Ji Weishi took his revolver out and pounded on the table. This was Secretary Ji's favorite ploy for stifling the opposition and encouraging the masses' fighting spirit. He raised his voice:

"Namby-pamby! You won't admit it? Take him away!"

Several guards who were stationed nearby rushed in around Zhou. That was the "organizational conclusion." The next act was the "mass denunciation." Having been a leader for several years, it would be hard not to have offended some people, but even as loudly as a few people shouted and screamed, the general meeting was surprisingly quiet.

It was then time for Secretary Ji to sum things up: the landlord element Zhou Jiajie had wormed his way into the Party, disrupted socialist construction, and committed a multitude of crimes. At this time, in response to the demands of the masses, he would be sentenced to perform supervised labor.[11] His last few words made the greatest impression on Zhou Jiajie: "Zhou Jiajie, listen to me: you can

---

11. "Supervised labor" (*jiandu laodong*) is a euphemism for work in a "labor reform" (*laogai*) camp.

forget about ever returning home in this life—unless every pot in your house rattles and shakes as you do!"

Ji Weishi was famous for his eloquence. A few short and forceful words had expressed everything he felt about struggle with the class enemy. After he finished speaking, he looked over to see Zhou Jiajie's reaction, then waved his arms in satisfaction to indicate that the meeting was over.

Zhou Jiajie was visibly stunned, his face deathly pale. He understood what Ji's words meant, "unless every pot in your house rattles and shakes . . . " He would never return home unless it was as a ghost. Vicious! Even in earlier struggle meetings against the landlords, Zhou Jiajie had never said anything like that. And besides, was it not an announcement of the death penalty? When was that ever a Party policy? . . . As he thought to himself, he looked around the meeting hall; at least his son had not come. He could see only his wife's back; she had drawn in her shoulders and seemed smaller and thinner than ever . . .

In a short while Zhou Jiajie was sent to West Ditch to "assemble for training." At that time he learned that with the exception of Chen Jiaci and a few others who were in college, all of the commune branch secretaries had become "evil persons"—even the commune director and two undersecretaries. All of these people were of poor peasant ancestry.

Everyday life at West Ditch consisted of three routines: hard labor, writing confessions, and holding struggle sessions—"evil people" struggling against "evil people." Confessions were written every day in exactly the same way. Struggle sessions were basically identical too: one person would stand on a bench and explain various "problems" while an audience of a couple hundred others would criticize and accuse him. The next day someone else would go up and the one who was accused the day before would then accuse others. It was certainly a case of "being both the target and the moving force of the revolution." It was nothing less than a theatrical farce, but every one of the "actors" was himself taking a tragic role: when they were chaotically and mechanically shouting, "You're not being honest!" or "Leniency to those who confess, severity for those who refuse!" every one of them felt an enormous sense of pity for the "protagonist" standing up there on the bench.

When no one else was near them, Zhou Jiajie quietly asked Lan

Jixuan—a former production brigade branch secretary who had only recently been nominated for commune undersecretary—what his problem was. At the end of 1960, Commune Secretary Ji Weishi had falsely reported, during a county-wide telephone conference call, a grain sale to the state of 275 tons. But later on he dumped his dirty water in Lan Jixuan's lap by saying Lan had made the false report. In that way Lan was branded a "sub-landlord" during the commune rectification drive.

Lan Jixuan and the recently branded "degenerate element" Liu Nancun (his crime was "placing evil persons in positions of importance"—he had allowed a man who had been a township official for several years before Liberation and another young man who had been pressed into the Nationalist Party's army to occupy positions as production team leaders) had worked together closely ever since land reform days. They had stayed up together many a night during that unforgettable year of 1958: sitting miserably through district and then commune meetings, trying to eke out a production target figure that would satisfy the district or county leadership, then carrying bamboo torches into a "night battle" for production. Finally, they went back to all-night commune meetings when they had to come up with a state grain requisition figure to satisfy county or commune leadership. In order to spur them on, they were brought before on-the-spot meetings: Look at such-and-such a brigade! Their grain stores are full to overflowing. How come you alone have no grain? You must be cheating on production figures and dividing it among yourselves! Everyone knew very well that the stores of the other brigades were full of straw with reed mats thrown over it and a thin layer of grain sprinkled on top to fool people. Someone had made a bitter joke about this: if only people's stomachs could pretend the same way—if filling them up with straw and tossing down a couple of grains of rice could prevent hunger—that would be wonderful.

In the middle of August, Zhou Jiajie's chief worry was: What is to become of the people now that power in Fangxing Commune has fallen into the hands of a man like Ji Weishi?

Cadres from the County Committee often came on assignments to West Ditch. From fragmentary reports Zhou Jiajie heard, he surmised that rural conditions did not seem to be improving, even though all of the "evil people" had already been locked up. On the contrary, the situation seemed to be growing more serious. Just after all of the "evil

people" were overthrown, the "swollen foot sickness" [malnutrition]
broke out all over the countryside.

IV

That was precisely the time when the people's beloved leader Comrade Peng Dehuai was toppled from power and Lin Biao took total
command of the armed forces after several years of convalescence. It
seems that there is a fixed amount of light in the universe. Just after
one star falls from the sky, another star shines with blinding
brightness.

Ji Weishi was a clever man, but his was a cleverness completely
opposite from Zhou Jiajie's. His feelings and thinking in response to
external events consistently took a completely different course from
Zhou's.

It was right in 1958 that he jumped all the way from credit union
director to commune secretary and then carried the "royal sword" of
the County Committee into the battle to "rectify" Fangxing Commune. Ji Weishi received the highest commendations from the
County Committee in 1958 and 1959. This single fact explains many
things.

In 1958—just at the time when cadres like Zhou Jiajie were beset by
physical and spiritual anxiety, were suffering from many internal
contradictions, going through repeated struggles, coming into direct
conflict with and incurring the dissatisfaction of the leadership, and
heading step by step toward destruction—Ji Weishi was as happy as a
fish discovering water: the "current situation" was molding him into
a "hero of our times."

From the tone of voice and subtle facial expressions of the County
Committee leaders, he very perceptively sensed the tenor of the
times. Thus he lost no opportunity to send up bold and loftily ambi-
tious plans, magnificent production targets, and outstanding figures
on the completion of state grain purchases. That was precisely the
time when those production brigade and commune cadres who did
not understand "the mission of the age" were frowning and sighing
all the time and revealing their "right-wing," "conservative," "nar-
row-minded peasant selfishness." Thus Ji Weishi's character stood
out heroically like an eagle among sparrows and attracted the particular attention and respect of the leadership.

At the grassroots level, whatever place Ji Weishi visited was immediately transformed from backward to progressive. His main point was always to get more money and food so that the masses would be easier to manipulate.

There were times, however, when some small misfortune would occur. Ji Weishi reported that the seedlings had been successfully planted slightly ahead of schedule, but when the County Committee investigated, the work was still far from finished. He reported grain sales to the state of 275 tons, but an investigation turned up a shortfall of 93.5 tons. That was easy to explain, of course: it was all the fault of the deputy secretary and the bookkeeper, who were careless with figures; "I did not check" this or "they didn't consult with me" on that. Ji Weishi had a pair of slippery shoulders, and responsibilities just naturally slid off them and onto those of his assistants. Ji Weishi's mistakes never involved anything more serious than "I didn't investigate thoroughly enough."

He only had one irremediable failing: he couldn't stand the scrutiny of thousands of pairs of eyes or the private evaluation and discussion of thousands of mouths. Once he realized what was happening and turned around to look, his expression, voice, and actions were completely different from those seen by the County Committee secretary. In 1959, a Dengshuang Commune member named Yuan Ping'an was eating in the threshing yard when Ji Weishi passed by (he was secretary of Dengshuang Commune at the time). Someone at the table called Ji Weishi over to eat with them, but Yuan Ping'an stopped him: "What're you calling him over to eat for? That bastard takes more and eats more; after he gets through with us, we won't even have enough potatoes to eat our fill!" Ji Weishi heard every word. That night Ji Weishi went to the production brigade to round up a few henchmen, told them to cut some tree branches, and announced that "we simply have to get rid of these unhealthy trends and evil practices!" Then he personally convened a meeting of all commune members and ordered Yuan Ping'an to confess: "What kind of trouble are you trying to stir up with all that fucking talk? What have you got against the People's Communes and the Three Red Banners?" When he didn't come clean, they tied him up. When he tried to explain himself again but did not make a full enough confession, four or five of Ji's henchmen tortured him with whips made of five tree branches tied together. At the same time an old man who had said the wheat was sown too closely together and a married couple who had dropped a few vegetable seeds during shipment received the same fierce beating.

Ji Weishi not only beat or cursed those he didn't like or who didn't like him. He also employed more "civilized" methods. For example, he once ordered a commune member to wear a big mud cake on his head and walk from one production brigade to another, "parading himself through the streets to expose his crimes to others" for five or six miles. The farthest production brigade had to check the mud cake on his arrival to make sure he hadn't moved it.

Actually the masses could see only a very small portion of Ji Weishi's true activities. All the rapid changes in production relations, the wild and chaotic work pace, the constant ups and downs in policy, just like sudden shifts in the earth's surface, naturally produced a number of cracks; and through these cracks Ji Weishi unceasingly sucked up oil and water [i.e., personal advantage]. And he had no qualms about the taste of human blood in what he sucked. During the great movement to produce homemade steel in residential back yards, every family was assessed two dollars. Accordingly, Ji Weishi had thousands of dollars in ready cash. Vast amounts of foodstuffs and material goods, together with several hundred state workers, were also at his disposal. When production brigades fell short on seeds and chemical fertilizer, another large sum of money passed through his hands. Tens of thousands of dollars in relief grain and workers' compensation were also under his control. He knew what sort of contacts he needed, and those people knew what they wanted from him, and thus everybody worked hand-in-hand to one another's advantage. It is still a mystery just exactly how much money he embezzled, how many things he stole, how much relief grain he sold for high prices at the market, or how much rice and lumber he secretly had shipped home. During the first Socialist Education Movement of 1963,[12] he was forced to confess to a certain figure, swearing he was "absolutely honest" and would "pay it back immediately"; but during the second Socialist Education Movement of 1965, he admitted to a much larger figure.

---

12. The Socialist Education Movement, also known as the Four Clean-ups Movement, was a nationwide campaign of political, economic, organizational, and ideological reform led by Mao Zedong and Lin Biao; widely considered a failure, it was also a prelude to the Cultural Revolution.

When all of the cadres of Fangxing Commune were cut down like grass and Ji Weishi became the commune secretary, he made an already calamitous situation even worse. It was as if the voices of all those cadres who had been forcibly silenced were concentrated in Ji Weishi's throat, so that this born orator now had a louder voice, a higher pitch, and much greater breath: "There aren't enough rations? Nonsense! The swollen foot sickness is nothing but the swollen foot sickness; it has nothing to do with hunger! State grain sales must be completed, and only ahead of schedule, never behind!"

Ji Weishi measured others by his own circumstances, and thus his words were not entirely lacking in sincerity. From 1959 on—at exactly the same time that the masses entered a state of semistarvation—Ji Weishi had fresh milk and eggs for breakfast every morning. He went to Fangxing Commune and used their crucible to decoct for himself special medicines that he wrote off as operating expenses, despite the fact that they were a disallowed item. He could go to the commune ponds whenever he liked and take home fresh fish; he could take free pork, duck eggs, and goose eggs; he could go to the old people's home or any of the production brigades and eat with them as often as he liked without paying anything . . . Matter becomes mind; thus it was quite excusable that he simply could not understand that there was such a thing as "starvation" in this world.

People now say, "If Ji Weishi had not come to Fangxing Commune that year, our losses would not have been so great." Obviously the role of the individual in history should still not be underestimated.

In Ji Weishi's dossier, however, the record of these "historical contributions" is unfortunately too brief. Look at his final evaluation: "This comrade is an activist worker, has great enthusiasm and spirit, and is able to thoroughly carry out the Party's policies and complete his every Party assignment. His class stand is resolute and his class view accurate; he is able to boldly carry out class struggle against evil people and their activities" (of course, that included Zhou Jiajie and those wronged ghosts of the nether world like Yuan Ping'an and others) . . . Ji Weishi's own assessment of himself is somewhat more detailed in its description of his "historic contributions": . . . standpoint resolute; always struggled against individualistic thought, discussion, or behavior; never wavered on the question of policy direction. While at Fangxing and Hua Jiao Communes, always resolutely struggled against the advocates of the household production contract system;[13] never wavered, never gave in, and took full responsibility for solving such problems."

All of these "resolute struggles" and so forth refer, of course, to his performance during the historical periods of 1958 to 1960 and 1962. But what about his embezzlement, stealing, beating and cursing of the masses, and false accusations of good people? There were two years when his evaluation read "engaged in embezzlement and stealing." This was written in the section on "shortcomings," but a "dialectical" change was also noted, and the "negations" of his various shortcomings also constituted "strong points": ". . . but he was able to confess voluntarily (?) and frankly (?), make just compensation, and make proper self-examination; and his work attitude was always correct (!)."

Thus, whenever the leadership of some commune was not forceful enough, Ji Weishi, "based on his political ability and integrity," would be sent "to strengthen the leadership and give full play to the Party's function as a revolutionary bulwark . . . etc., etc."

None of this is at all surprising, considering that by 1966 Ji Weishi's dossier no longer contained the slightest hint of wrongdoing. His thinking and his virtue were both pure and unblemished; his only minor fault was that "on occasion he is rather one-sided in his evaluation of certain problems; he lacks thoroughness and attention to details in his style of work, etc."

Why did those comrades sitting in their County Committee Organization Office writing such evaluations never go down and look around? Why did they never go to the production brigades, the grassroots cadres, and the commune members and listen to what they had to say? For example:

"Flattering toward the leaders, but arrogant and oppressive toward the workers . . ."

"He's an expert liar; always reports good news, never bad; always reports unfinished work as having been completed ahead of schedule."

---

13. The "household production contract system" (*baochan daohu*), now generally translated in *Beijing Review* as the "responsibility system," is the "pragmatic" farm policy in which individual households, the smallest units of rural organization, are responsible for contracts that they make with the state and are paid more money if they exceed their contracts. During the Cultural Revolution this form of "material incentive" to work was viewed as "taking the capitalist road."

"A small man with a big head (a self-important official). His word alone is law."

"Always cursing, beating, and locking people up or sending them to do forced labor for the commune."

The simplest and most devastating evaluation was: "He gets ahead by climbing over the dead bodies of the masses—totally without shame!"

The only weapon that the masses, who could always see things clearly, could use against such a man was to despise and ignore him. They would greet anyone on the street, but somehow "didn't see" this particular corpus of flesh and blood.

The position a man occupies in the hearts of the masses can actually be greatly at odds with the position he occupies among the ranks of officials.

V

Working all day with the commune members and living at home with his family, Zhou Jiajie could not really be considered isolated; but spiritually he was living far away on a very small island, an island so small that there was room only for him alone to dwell there.

Among the masses he was regarded almost as a recluse, and everyone gradually got used to ignoring his existence. Sometimes this made him feel very bad, but it also gave him an important opportunity—he could hear things that other people couldn't, and he was extremely interested in every piece of intelligence about the outside world. Such news was related to his personal security and to his hope of someday returning to normal life.

He had already fallen to the status of the lowest of the low. He was politically equal to landlords, rich peasants, counterrevolutionaries, and other bad elements, but he lacked even their ability to speak and thus suffered more fear and anxiety than they did. He lived in constant fear of falling into some sort of trap. All he wished for was to avoid harassment, accusations, and beatings . . .

His fears were, of course, not unfounded. Whenever he collected manure with the other commune members, even though he had carried six loads, the brigade leader would mark him down for only four loads while marking everyone else down for six loads. The others would receive four work points, but he, only three. He was extremely angry, but could not speak; he could only force himself to calm down and let it go. Nevertheless, the brigade leader noticed his dissatisfaction and cursed him: "You're only acting crazy!" At that he became over-excited, forgot himself, jumped up, and beat violently on his own chest. The brigade leader took a close look at him, thought a moment, and said, "You're only pretending to be a crazy fool. If we gave you a beating, you'd talk all right!"

He couldn't sleep at all that night, he was so angry with himself for losing his composure. It was clear now that the brigade leader already suspected him of only pretending to be deaf and dumb. He must be extremely cautious.

He went on to consider that merely pretending to be completely deaf and dumb was not sufficient. He had to build the walls of his little island even higher and plan thoroughly for any eventuality. When a couple of close friends who had unreliable class backgrounds paid him one of their frequent visits, he wrote a note to his son: "In the future, these kinds of people should not come very often." After that, in order to protect himself he decided not to associate with three kinds of people: cadres, people with political problems, and people who were too clever for anyone's good.

His wife and son were talking about buying a radio. At first he thought this would be a good idea to liven up his family's silent world and give them some relief from boredom, but when his son wrote him a note asking for his opinion, he wrote down very clearly: "We cannot do it! Didn't you see what happened to Zhou Zhongci?" That was the end of that.

Zhou Zhongci was a nephew. He had been branded a rightist in 1958 because he said the peasants did not have enough to eat. He was later sent to work at the Mianyang Agricultural Machinery Station. There was a radio there with a loudspeaker system attached. On one occasion he tired of listening to a political program and turned the dial to a music station. An alarm sounded for thirty seconds and the security forces immediately came running. Zhou Zhongci was arrested on the spot for the crime of secretly listening to and rebroadcasting an "enemy station." He was relieved of his duties, sentenced to three years in prison, and branded an active counterrevolutionary. When he came out of prison, he was sent back to the countryside to perform supervised labor.

Besides, Zhou Jiajie reasoned, since they already suspect that I am pretending to be mute, they will believe I harbor resentment and will suspect me of sitting at home plotting some sort of activity to get back at them. In those days any radio could be declared to be a wireless sending and receiving set, not to mention the simple fact that if his family bought a radio they would suspect all the more that he was only pretending deafness . . . He closed his doors to all guests, didn't buy a radio, didn't go to market, and reduced his contacts with the outside world to an absolute minimum. He could do without all things but one—security.

He would close his door at night and sit there weaving basket after basket out of thin strips of bamboo. In two evenings he could weave a pair of baskets, and his son could sell them for a few cents in the marketplace. This was his only recreation and entertainment.

He was the earliest one up every morning. He would first sweep up the entire little yard until it was perfectly clean from wall to fence and outside his gate; then he would start a fire and cook breakfast. He also had to decide when it was time to sell something in the marketplace and what they should buy there as well; he would record everything very clearly in his account book . . . He had voluntarily taken over the management of all the household affairs and housework. He did so not merely to occupy his mind and relieve some of his depression. In his home he felt like a human being: he could think, organize, arrange, and direct things, instead of silently, passively, and mechanically following everyone else in the completion of this or that labor assignment.

After two or three years he finally became accustomed to being deaf and dumb. People said that he had regained some weight and that his complexion had improved. Of course, he did not have to participate in any meetings and did not have to worry about anything in the commune or the brigade; he was as relaxed as could be. Any very attentive person, however, could see that his expression was becoming duller day by day. Compared to the former Zhou Jiajie, who was full of talk and laughter and whose happiness, anger, grief, and joy were immediately registered on his face, he had become another person.

His own acclimation to the role of being deaf and dumb came more slowly than his general acceptance as such by others. In any public gathering, he himself no longer made any demands for expression or association; but in his heart, his inability to speak up was still a constant source of pain.

The process of being forced to cut himself off from other people and become isolated was the exact opposite of the experience of Sichuan's famous "white-haired girl," Luo Changxiu.[14] When Luo Changxiu escaped into the mountains at the age of fourteen, she immediately cut off all contact with the outside world and became absolutely isolated. She heard only the sound of wind and rain and the cries of tigers and wolves, but not the sound of human voices. She no longer had opportunities to express her thoughts, wishes, or feelings to other people, and thus she naturally came to abandon the desire to do so. Zhou Jiajie, on the other hand, was already a mature adult of thirty-six and had been working in society for many years. He had lived in a rapidly changing society and, as a consequence of his wide contacts with other people, his "social nature" was more highly developed than that of most of the masses. His contacts with other people were abruptly cut off under these quite different circumstances, and yet he still had to live all the time in the midst of the same social group. His ears were continually providing him with various bits of intelligence, which filtered through his mind and immediately became a part of his own thoughts and feelings; but he could not convey any information or express even the slightest reaction to the events of the outside world. Most human beings probably have occasion to endure such painful circumstances only once in their lifetimes—during that brief moment when they are very near death and their mental faculties are still quite lucid but they have lost the ability to speak. Zhou Jiajie, however, had to live under these circumstances all the time. Thus, for him to accustom himself to not speaking was several times more difficult than it was for Luo Changxiu; just as Luo Changxiu could not get used to speaking, did not want to, and was not very good at it once she had returned to the human world.

The written word became Zhou Jiajie's only means of communication with other people, but written words cannot take the place of speech. Whenever an old friend came to visit, Zhou Jiajie naturally wanted to chat a bit with him, yet it was imperative that he not open his mouth. Could written notes possibly serve the same purpose?

When he was feeding the hogs, they knocked over a pail of grain

---

14. Luo Changxiu is the protagonist of the story "The White-Haired Girl" (Baimaonü).

husks, and his wife scolded him at length: "A grown man like you, and you can't even hold the grain pail steady!" He was both excited and angry and wanted to shout something right back at her, but he couldn't. Writing a note was out of the question, because she was illiterate.

He was very upset with his son about something, so he wrote a very short little note: "Silly little fool!" His daughter-in-law saw it, thought it referred to her, and went off crying. He had no way of explaining the misunderstanding; after all, he was not even supposed to be able to hear her sobbing.

Aside from note writing, he could only employ facial expressions and gestures. His wife and daughter-in-law were constantly quarreling. His daughter-in-law, of course, had no compunction about criticizing her mother-in-law in front of her deaf father-in-law. Zhou Jiajie had wanted to interfere for a long time but was completely powerless. One day at dinner when his daughter-in-law was carrying on again, he gave her a dark disapproving look, but it was no use. In a fit of rage, he knocked over the dining table in order to assert his authority as the head of the household.

VI

In 1972, something very important happened.

One day Zhou Zhongci came running over to Zhou Jiajie's house and began gesturing excitedly this way and that. Zhou Jiajie finally understood him: somebody had fallen to his death from a high place. But who was it? Zhou Zhongci pointed to his head, with the meaning that the person was bald. Khrushchev? He had fallen from power long ago; Zhou Zhongci wouldn't be so excited about his death. Zhou Zhongci was growing a little impatient. He tried to imitate the person's facial expression and way of walking, but it wasn't until he pretended to wave the *Quotations from Chairman Mao* that Zhou Jiajie realized who it was: Oh, Lin Biao!

He had not read the newspapers for three years, but from that day on he went out to the roadside every day to wait for the postman and be the first one to see the newspapers.

As his feeling of personal security grew stronger, he gradually began to think beyond his own individual safety and well-being. He felt as if something was vaguely stirring within him, as if something inside him that had been dormant for many years was gradually beginning to reawaken . . .

It was 1972 already, but the production brigade's per acre grain production had not yet even matched the figures for 1953, when they had developed the first-stage cooperatives! The brigade leader wore out his whistle urging people on to work harder, but everyone was lazy and malingering. They were very good at producing children though! There was not enough to eat then, so what were they going to eat in the future? "If they would make me Party branch secretary, I would . . ." The first time that thought occurred to Zhou Jiajie, it surprised him, but later on his thoughts often tended in that direction.

He turned forty that year. Perhaps it would be his lucky year. He had only worked for the Party six years, but he'd already been a criminal for twelve.

A dark shadow often rose up in his memory and would not allow him to be optimistic. It was something that had occurred in 1962 when he was not yet a mute. He had been cutting down some creepers when a cadre from County Central came up beside him, took his arm, and whispered softly, "I think making you an alien class element was an unjust verdict. They're just beginning to reexamine some cases at the county level. I think there's some hope for you . . ."

From then on, every time county or commune cadres came to the production brigade, Zhou Jiajie would glance at them hopefully. Maybe they've come to find me? Or perhaps they've come to check up on my performance these last few years? Or to reinvestigate my family's economic condition before Land Reform?

In that year there really were thousands of good comrades whose cases were reexamined and who were then readmitted to the Party or given their former jobs back. There were even a few in Xinjin County. It seems that Zhou Jiajie's case was brought up, but the only result was that a few more words were added to his dossier: "A correct decision, no need for reexamination."

A new hope burst forth in 1975. A very great hope indeed, related to the reappearance of the name Deng Xiaoping. News of a "Party reform" came shortly after that, and there were constant rumors that new rural and personnel policies would soon be implemented. At that point the desire that Zhou Jiajie had nurtured in his heart for seven long years, the desire to escape from being deaf and dumb and to speak out once again, was stronger than ever before.

The following year, he passed a note to his son: "Find a good doctor; I want to be cured."

On the basis of the overall national situation, he had concluded that if he was "cured" at this time, even if there were some suspicion that he had been faking, no one would investigate him. He still had a strong hope lodged deep in his heart: one of these days someone may come to ask about the injustices I've suffered; at that time, I'll have to be able to speak.

His son and his close friends did in fact go to a great deal of trouble to make an appointment with a good doctor for him, but they were unsuccessful. That winter, the situation once again took a turn for the worse. First came the "counterattack against the reversal of rightist verdicts,"[15] and then the death of Premier Zhou Enlai plunged the entire nation into deep sorrow and anxiety.

Zhou Jiajie hid in a deserted place for fear that someone would find him weeping, and the dark clouds weighed all the more heavily on his heart. Why talk about "curing" his illness? What hope was there to clear up his political problem? China's historical clock seemed to have stopped again.

Who could have imagined that the pent-up anger, resentment, and enmity that had been growing steadily in the hearts of all the Chinese people was just about to coalesce into a mighty force that would sweep the Gang of Four and their followers into the graveyard of history?

VII

After the fall of the Gang of Four, Zhou Jiajie continued to keep silent for almost three more years. Could this be because suffering and apprehension had weighed on his heart so long that his spirit had already become as frozen and numb as the expression on his face? After the slogans "Down with the Gang of Four" and "Liberate the people" had joyfully resounded for so long, why was he still so

---

15. This was an attack by the Gang of Four on Deng Xiaoping and others who were trying to exonerate many cadres wrongly accused or imprisoned as "rightists" during the Cultural Revolution.

unmoved that he did not stand up and shout out his appeal for a redress of grievances?

Our wishes always travel in a straight line, while history often prefers a tortuous course. The martyred Shi Yunfeng, who so bravely opposed Lin Biao and the Gang of Four, could never have imagined that he would die at the hands of the Gang of Four element Wang Huaixiang long after the Gang themselves had been smashed.[16] Just think about a few things: Remember when the verdict on the Tiananmen Incident was finally reversed.[17] Remember that as much as two years after the Gang of Four had fallen from the historical stage, some people still refused to allow discussion of the "extreme left" line and many people who had opposed that line were still being punished in prison as "active counterrevolutionaries." Remember again that as late as 1979 the slogan "Practice is the sole criterion of truth"[18] was still meeting a great deal of opposition . . . When one recalls all these things, Zhou Jiajie's continued wait-and-see attitude of silence does not seem strange at all.

After October 1976 [when the Gang of Four were arrested], he once again waited on the road every day for the postman to deliver the newspapers. He listened greedily to every word people said and carefully and unblinkingly observed every little change in their daily lives as well as their every reaction to these changes and their expectations for even greater and more complete change.

---

16. Shi Yunfeng was a student at East China Normal University in Shanghai who became nationally famous in the late 1970s because of his arrest and trial for opposing the extremist ideology of the Cultural Revolution and, in particular, the cult of Party Chairman Mao Zedong. At the direction of Peng Chong, second secretary of the Municipal Party Committee in Shanghai and member of the Central Politburo, Shi was executed for his "political crimes," even though, with the overthrow of the Gang of Four, the politics that Shi opposed were already well on their way to official repudiation. Shi's case became a cause célèbre among intellectuals and political moderates, but was discussed only "internally" (neibu) until 1981, when Shi was officially exonerated. To mention the case publicly in March 1980, as Liu Binyan does here, required courage.

17. Tiananmen is the Gate of Heavenly Peace in Beijing that stands before the vast Tiananmen Square, which is symbolic of the political center of China. The Tiananmen Incident refers to April 5, 1976, when hundreds of thousands of people gathered in the square in a spontaneous tribute to Premier Zhou Enlai. Zhou had died January 8, 1976, and April 5 was the occasion of the Qingming Festival, when Chinese sweep family gravesites and make obeisances to the departed. The crowd had gathered in an antitotalitarian spirit, but was forcibly driven away and the demonstration declared "counterrevolutionary." The "verdict was reversed" on the incident in December 1978, when the Beijing Municipal Party Committee declared the demonstration "revolutionary."

18. This slogan, together with that of "Liberate thinking," was put forth by the Third Plenum of December 1978 and is associated with the "pragmatic" approach of Deng Xiaoping.

The first joyful event was Comrade Deng Xiaoping's return to work. Many large and small followers of Lin Biao and the Gang of Four were either arrested or removed from office, and that made people feel both relieved and happy. Everyone was talking about Comrade Zhao Ziyang leading a group of Provincial Committee cadres down to the villages to make an extended examination of local conditions and to solicit the opinions and listen to the demands of the peasants and the rural cadres. The people were finally beginning to reap real benefits: whether or not to practice double cropping of rice was no longer an issue of revolution or counterrevolution; they no longer had to hear "If wet rice won't do, plant dry wheat," and "Late autumn is a good time for wheat. . ."[19] Long-awaited reforms in the cropping system arrived. "Dazhai-style work points"[20] were eliminated, and the principle of more pay for more work was reinstated, as was self-regulation for production brigades. The state put into practice a whole system of reforms that were beneficial to the peasants and allowed them to enrich themselves through their own labor . . .

"Party Central knows . . ." Zhou Jiajie nodded his head in silent approval as he talked to himself, ". . . knows what sort of errors have occurred these past years, knows how the peasants feel and what they have suffered. Just look, even while the nation is experiencing such difficulties, they're still raising the state purchase price for agricultural products; they're really taking good care of us peasants . . ."

He paid particular attention to the fact that the slogan "Take class struggle as the key" was not mentioned, and that one unjust case after another was being reversed. It looked like they were proceeding from the near to the distant, first taking care of the 1970s, then later the 1960s and 1950s . . . His heart was slowly warming up, and the flame of hope that had been put out so often before was flaring up once more.

He still did not dare give free rein to his hopes, however, because policies had fluctuated back and forth too many times during the past few years. Who could guarantee that the brakes would not suddenly be applied again? Weren't conditions just like this in 1959, 1962, and

---

19. During the Cultural Revolution, Party leaders forced the peasants against their better judgment to plant grain sprouts too close together and to plant land with grain even when it was not suitable. As a result, good land was harmed and production fell.

20. Dazhai, in Shanxi Province, was a model agricultural commune during the Cultural Revolution. Its work-point system gave peasants credit for "political behavior" and de-emphasized individual material incentives. After the Cultural Revolution it was revealed that Dazhai's vaunted accomplishments had been staged with state support.

1975? And besides, for so many years every movement had been "anti-rightist," never "anti-leftist." Supposing somebody jumped out again and started shouting, "All of you are rightists and have to be completely rectified!"—wouldn't that be the end of everything? He was also worried that when it came time to exonerate him, since everyone knew he was deaf and dumb someone would say, "What's a person like him worth? Forget him!" One statement like that and he might be confined to oblivion again, just like back in 1962.

Thus he continued to wait and see, continued to remain silent, and continued to stifle his overly ardent hopes. He was afraid of the shock of disappointment.

The Goddess of Fortune finaliy remembered this man who had been forgotten for twenty years.

On the morning of January 4, 1979, the whole family was in the living room after breakfast when Zhou's eldest son, Zhou Xinqiang, said very thoughtfully, "Something very strange happened. Yesterday afternoon, when I was coming home from work, I ran into Production Brigade Secretary Qin, and he asked me several times, 'Can your father really hear and speak or not?' . . . Something may be going on."

Naturally, Zhou Jiajie "didn't hear" what his son said. He thought the time had probably arrived, but did not dare to act rashly. He had to find someone to consult with and see what was going on.

He immediately thought of Chen Jiaci, a man of similar age, experience, and cultural level, who had been one of his best friends in the early days. He had also been a Party branch secretary in 1959, and if he hadn't gone to study at Dujiang University he would have suffered the same evil fate as Zhou Jiajie. During the most dangerous days of the Cultural Revolution, he was the only one who dared to visit Zhou Jiajie's home and to write notes asking about the wellbeing of his family and if they had any problems . . . Zhou Jiajie wrote a note and sent Xinqiang off to find Chen Jiaci. He was a person you could rely on, and it wouldn't matter if you asked him something you shouldn't.

Without waiting for Xinqiang to speak, Chen Jiaci put down his seed potatoes, wiped his hands, and asked, "Did you come to talk about your father's case?" Xinqiang was both surprised and pleased as he quickly answered, "My dad told me to come and ask Uncle

Chen if his case could be brought up now." Chen Jiaci was quite positive. "Why not? Of course it's time to bring it up! You go home and tell him I'll come over this noon; otherwise tonight for sure."

At noontime Chen Jiaci came to the Zhou home and another conversation written on notes took place. "When your case was first handled, what was the verdict?" "Alien class element. Exaggeration of production figures leading to rural starvation. Misusing over seventy dollars of public money. Embezzling twenty dollars." Chen Jiaci took a brush and painted lines through "alien class element" and "exaggeration . . ." These two lines were like two crowbars prying up a large heavy stone that had been weighing down Zhou Jiajie's heart for twenty years. Under "misusing . . ." Chen Jiaci wrote, "returned year by year; no longer counts." Under "embezzling . . ." he wrote, "Even if it were true, it's not serious enough for such a verdict."

The next day Chen Jiaci returned, bringing with him Yang Shuncheng, who had been the deputy secretary of Fangxing Commune and was now the deputy director of its grain office. Zhou Jiajie set out some wine and they carried on another paper conversation as they drank. Chen Jiaci wrote, "Unjust cases are currently being reversed all over the country; your case can probably be cleared up. Can you speak or not? If you've been pretending, you can just give us a sign and we can, if you like, keep your secret until after your case is resolved."

That was the longest question Zhou Jiajie had ever been asked in his eleven years of silent conversations, and it was the one that caused him the greatest hesitation. After some time, he finally took up the brush and wrote, "Thank you for your help. I'm afraid that I will not explain myself clearly."

Chen Jiaci looked at the note and stared at Zhou Jiajie for a long time, until the tears welled up in his eyes. The grave injustice suffered by this beloved childhood friend who stood before him, plus the almost indescribable pain that he himself had endured these past years, all pressed at once on his heavy heart. At the same time, he felt a great elation in finally proving that Zhou Jiajie was really pretending to be mute and that now he had a chance to start a new life in this world that had recently grown lovable again.

On the sixth of January, the County Committee called a meeting of third-level cadres. There Zhou Jiajie's note was delivered to the County Committee secretary, Comrade Zhong Guanglin. Zhong

Guanglin had long ago heard about someone called Zhou Jiajie. From the words "I'm afraid that I will not explain myself clearly," he inferred that Zhou probably could speak. He ordered the Organization Department to check his case file. The Commune Cadre Committee and the Organization Department cadres examined the original verdict point by point and found that not one point could hold water. They determined that Zhou Jiajie's father was not a landlord; he had merely hired some temporary laborers and sold some wine at the county market. The so-called misuse of public money was only Zhou Jiajie's borrowing one or two dollars when he had to go to the district township for meetings, and he had paid it all back later out of his wages. But the embezzlement of twenty dollars was retained in the new adjudication.

County Secretary Zhong asked Fangxing Commune Secretary Li Shuquan to call Zhou Jiajie to the county seat. Zhou's son brought him to town on his bicycle, and Li Shuquan told him, "Your situation has been discussed several times and we've decided it is an unjust case." Zhou Jiajie's heart was pounding like storm-blown waves, but his facial muscles retained their by now habitual lack of expression. He did not speak either—this too was a years-old habit that did not require the least bit of control. "He can't hear," his son explained quite sincerely, and another written conversation ensued. Zhou Jiajie wrote, "Wait until I am cured and then we can talk." Li Shuquan wrote, "I'll give you three days to be cured." The two men looked at each other closely, each one contemplating his next move.

Zhang Qunfang, a female cadre from Fangxing Commune, was standing nearby witnessing this bizarre confrontation. This young, straightforward, and able comrade had already figured out Zhou Jiajie's true situation and felt great sympathy for him. Watching Zhou Jiajie's face blushing red and then turning pale again, she could no longer bear to see him go on suffering so; she walked over, shook his hand warmly, and spoke in a friendly voice, "Don't worry any more. It's a new day! You still think you can't speak clearly enough? None of us needs to be afraid any more." Zhou Jiajie seemed visibly moved, but he was still full of anxious reservations and stood there as speechless as before. Li Shuquan and Zhang Qunfang found it extremely difficult to wait there patiently for him to speak his first words. For a full ten minutes the only movement was that of large beads of sweat pouring down Zhou Jiajie's face. Finally he stood up; he had decided to speak, but his tongue was very heavy and sluggish. Tears choked his throat as he barely and haltingly forced out three rather indistinct syllables:

"I . . . . . can . . . . . speak!" This was the first thing he had said in eleven years.

The strange thing was that the apprehension he had felt for twenty long years still clung to him as if from inertia. At that moment Zhou Jiajie had already escaped from his many anxieties, but his mind and tongue were still not working in harmony, and he just kept repeating the refrain that had rung in his head so many hundreds of times: "I'm afraid . . . I will not explain myself clearly."

The room was completely silent except for the sound of his son weeping for joy and sadness.

"I was afraid . . ."—it was an historic echo. The sound of his son's weeping was a fitting end to twenty tragic years of his family history.

"I never thought I'd see this day!" Zhou Jiajie confided to his son on the way home. The sounds of rejoicing were interspersed with the sounds of sighs, and unprecedented happiness accompanied feelings about a past too painful to recall. In the spring of 1979, all over the length and breadth of China, innumerable people were repeating that same short but profoundly significant sentence, "I never thought I'd see this day!" It marked the end of an era for an individual and for an entire nation, and announced the beginning of a new historical epoch.

On the road home, there were the same long lines of people and vehicles, the same wheat fields, and the same rows of flowering rape and beans; but Zhou Jiajie felt differently about all of them. When he left he was a longtime stranger to all of those things; but now as he returned to this world after a long exile, he was once more an equal member of society, one of those people walking, driving, and working there. He was once more a human being living in the human world.

His son began to pedal faster in his excitement to carry the great good news to their family. The road was quite uneven and they bounced up and down terribly. "Running proudly in the spring wind, the horse's hooves fly . . ." It had been so long since Zhou Jiajie had sung, but now he truly felt like singing a song; yet when he recalled how difficult it was just to speak and how bad he sounded, he decided not to spoil his present mood.

An acquaintance they met on the road used his customary gestures to ask Zhou Jiajie where he had been. Zhou Jiajie jumped down off the bicycle and said, "We went into Xinjin County Seat." The fellow stood there stunned for a moment before he finally asked, "Who cured you?" That question caused Zhou Jiajie some consternation. How should he put it? He should thank Party Central, but it was too large, so he finally answered, "Commune Secretary Li cured me."

The whole family was sitting in the front yard waiting and hoping that their wishes would be fulfilled when the head of the household went into the city to be exonerated. If that were to happen the whole family could breathe freely again and hold their heads high once more.

Zhou Jiajie's daughter ran through the gate. His granddaughter ran into his arms. Zhou Jiajie hugged her tightly and, mustering all the strength at his command, uttered the two words: "Good———granddaughter!" He could feel that his eyes were wet again.

Everyone was dumbfounded. Zhou Jiajie looked over at his wife; two long streaks of tears were streaming down her dry, bony cheeks . . .

VIII

Zhou Jiajie returned once again to his position of twenty years before as production brigade Party branch secretary. His current possession of power was due not to any empty slogan or falsely inflated production figures, but to his ability to work the brigade's land for the genuine and substantial benefit of the people living there. When he finally put plow to earth, however, he discovered that the land was not what it used to be. He had not only to plow the fields, but also to bend over constantly to pick up many stones and to pull up deep-rooted congo grass. Out of the twenty-one Party members in his production brigade, only five were the kind who could get things moving. The population had increased greatly, but the arable land had actually decreased . . .

Zhou Jiajie was not one to remain idle. Enough garbage had piled up on this piece of land since he had left the scene that he would have all he could do to clean it up.

Things wouldn't be easy for Zhou Jiajie, either. The first time he opened his mouth to speak, a most unhappy event occurred. A very well-known person walked over from the far side of the room where

Zhou's exoneration had been announced. Zhou Jiajie quickly smiled and held out his hand, but the man just turned his face and walked away. It was Ji Weishi.

Perhaps Ji Weishi was not yet accustomed to the new atmosphere of the times and imagined that he sensed something unpropitious in it. He and a few others like him had gotten so accustomed to hearing only the sound of their own voices that they could not enjoy a hubbub of many voices.

But old man history tells us that it's better to be a little more noisy. A silent era cannot be a good one.

Contributors

Michael S. Duke is Assistant Professor of Modern Chinese at the University of British Columbia. He received his doctorate from the University of California, Berkeley, in 1975, and has taught at George Washington University, University of Vermont, University of Wisconsin, and National Taiwan University. His publications include *Lu Yu* (Twayne, 1977) and many scholarly articles and translations in both traditional and modern Chinese literature.

James V. Feinerman is a lawyer (J.D., Harvard Law School, 1979) as well as a scholar of Chinese literature (Ph.D., Yale University, 1979). During 1979–80 he studied Chinese literature at Beijing University and did research on law in affiliation with the Institute of Law, Chinese Academy of Social Sciences. From there he went to New York as an associate at the law firm of Davis Polk & Wardwell. In 1982 he returned on a Fulbright fellowship to Beijing University, Department of Law.

Leo Ou-fan Lee is Professor of Chinese literature at the University of Chicago. He has also taught at Dartmouth College, the Chinese University of Hong Kong, Princeton University, and Indiana University. He is author of *The Romantic Generation of Modern Chinese Writers* (Harvard, 1973) as well as many articles in both English and Chinese on modern Chinese literature and culture. He has edited several collections, including *The Lyrical and the Epic: Studies of Modern Chinese Literature* by Jaroslav Průšek (Indiana, 1980).

Perry Link is Associate Professor of Oriental Languages at UCLA, where he specializes in modern Chinese literature. He has taught Chinese language at Harvard University, Middlebury College, and Princeton University. During 1979–80 he was in China doing research on contemporary literature. He is interested in popular thought and is author of *Mandarin Ducks and Butterflies* (California, 1981).

John Rohsenow is Assistant Professor of Linguistics at the University of Illinois at Chicago Circle. In 1979–80 he taught linguistics and American literature at Hangzhou University and in 1980–81 did research at Nanjing University on aspect in Chinese syntax.

Madelyn Ross became interested in Chinese literature while doing an undergraduate thesis on Ding Ling at Princeton University. During 1979–80 she studied modern Chinese literature at Fudan University in Shanghai. She is currently working on an M.A. in Chinese economics at Columbia University.

Kyna Rubin received her M.A. in modern Chinese literature from the University of British Columbia in 1979 and then spent a year studying at Fudan University in Shanghai. Her "Interview with Wang Ruowang" appears in *China Quarterly* no. 87 (September 1981).